OUR GG IN HAVANA

Our GG in Havana

PEDRO JUAN GUTIÉRREZ

Translated by
JOHN KING

faber and faber

First published in 2004 by
Editorial Anagrama, Spain
First published in this translation in 2010
by Faber and Faber Ltd
Bloomsbury House
74–77 Great Russell Street
London WC1B 3DA

Typeset by Faber and Faber
Printed in England by JF Print, Sparkford, Somerset

A CIP record for this book
is available from the British Library

ISBN 978-0-571-23027-3

2 4 6 8 10 9 7 5 3 1

I think that trying to be a writer is a very dangerous business.

John Cheever, *The Journals,* 1979

Thought's a luxury. Do you think the peasant sits
and thinks of God and Democracy when he gets
inside his mud hut at night?

Graham Greene, *The Quiet American*

(remark by Fowler)

1

A Pan Am four-engined Clipper, coming from Chicago, entered Havana airspace from the southeast. It descended smoothly, lined up the main runway and, at 1.10 p.m., landed at the small airport of Rancho Boyeros. It was a summer day, cloudy, humid and extremely hot.

A group of around forty happy, carefree American tourists, some dressed in flowery shirts and white trousers, got quickly through passport control. The official took a few more seconds with a short, thin man who had a British passport. He checked the photo, looked at the man's face, saw that they were identical, stamped the entry date and said in a friendly manner: 'Welcome, mister.'

The small man left the airport building and several taxi drivers offered their services. He did not look at them. He got into the nearest taxi. In a rudimentary Spanish he said to the driver:

'Can you take me to a hotel in the city?'

'Do you want a luxury hotel?'

'No.'

'There are comfortable hotels around Central Park and it's a good location.'

'I don't know the city.'

'Are you American? Maybe you'd like . . ?'

'I'm not American, I'm British.'

'Well then, the best place for you is the Hotel Inglaterra. They have good rates and it's very comfortable.'

'Fine.'

The taxi driver kept chatting on: about the heat, the area around Central Park, Major League baseball, the local dishes that he could eat in restaurants. He jumped from one topic to the next, without pausing for a second. The visitor did not respond. Despite this, the driver kept on talking very loudly, almost shouting, so that he could be heard above the car radio, which was tuned to a station that mixed shrill advertisements with guarachas, chachachas, rumbas, mambo and rancheras. A bit of everything.

That incessant noise, the heat and the sticky humidity, the excessive tropical light, the dizzying traffic along Boyeros Avenue and the lack of sleep on the long journey from Liverpool combined to make the visitor feel ill. He was nauseous. He reacted brusquely:

'Please, be quiet.'

'Shall I turn off the radio?'

'Yes, and I'd like total quiet. I'm feeling ill.'

'Oh, sorry.'

The man huddled on the back seat and shut his eyes. He'd come looking for excitement and a radical change of scene. Perhaps – why not – a radical life change. He would never do it in Liverpool. In another place, he might well be able to start out in a new direction.

A few minutes later the taxi stopped in front of the Hotel Inglaterra. A uniformed doorman opened the door for him and took him to reception. The receptionist greeted him politely in English and offered him one of the luxury suites. The man looked at him coldly and said tersely:

'A single, inexpensive room.'

'Very good, sir.'

The receptionist opened the register and asked:

'Your name and nationality, please.'

'Mister Greene, British.'

3

He handed his passport across at the same time. The receptionist's face lit up. He beamed and took a book from under the counter. He showed it to him: *The Shipwrecked.* And he said:

'I'm reading this. I love it. I have read all your books. Your English is exquisite. I learn a lot.'

GG gave him a sardonic smile.

'It is an honour for the hotel, Mister Greene. I will give you room 305, which has a large balcony and an excellent view of Central Park.'

'Many thanks.'

'And if you will allow me, as a welcoming present, I'll send you up a bottle of . . . what do you prefer, gin or Scotch?'

'Scotch.'

'This is just for our distinguished guests. It is an honour to have you here . . . umm . . . I don't want to bother you, but could you sign the book for me?'

He wrote on the first page: 'For a friend. GG, 15 July 1955. Havana.'

The bellboy took him to his room on the third floor. It was a luxury hotel, with enamel tiles on the wall, embossed ceilings, elegant cane furniture, pleasant muted lighting and deep green plants in every corner. It was quiet, peaceful and smelled of lavender. GG felt very good. The place had class. The bellboy, a thin and not very young black man, moved slowly. There was no hurry. He opened the door to the room and placed GG's bag in the wardrobe. He opened the curtains and the doors to the balcony – and suddenly there was a torrential downpour. The man smiled and said:

'That's good, it'll get cooler.'

GG put his hand in his pocket and gave him some coins. The man left immediately. The city was even more beautiful in the rain. He looked at the view for several minutes. He felt that the air was getting cooler and cleaner. There was a knock on the door. They'd brought him a silver tray with a bottle of Scotch, ice, soda and glasses. He poured out a generous measure, with a touch of soda and two ice cubes, and smiling, relaxed, he looked out at the drenched city and gave a toast to himself:

'Welcome to Havana, Mister Greene. You are our honoured guest.'

2

GG is dozing on the plane and suddenly feels a violent shuddering. He looks out of the window to his right and sees with horror the wing falling apart in the middle of a storm, with lightning and thick black clouds. A second later all that is left is the frame, its metal supports all twisted. The Clipper is plunging down. Everyone is screaming, terrified, but there is no time for anything. The plane is sinking in the ocean. It floats down to hell in the cold and the darkness. GG is a small boy and the water is coming in through his mouth and nose and it's drowning him. He's a child without any strength. He can do nothing. It is terribly dark and he knows that he is drowning. He can no longer breathe. He drowns.

He woke up with his arms waving, unable to breathe. Finally he opened his eyes and breathed in. He filled his lungs. He cried. He was that child.

No. Not any more. He sat up in bed. He closed his eyes and the plane enveloped in flames appeared before him. He opened his eyes, terrified, and went across to the balcony to get some fresh air. It was dark. And there was a slight breeze.

He finally returned to reality. He served himself a Scotch with ice and soda. He drank it quickly and felt hungry. Nine in the evening. He had slept enough. He went to the bathroom. He washed his hands and face and went down to the hotel restaurant. It was very nice, but too elegant and expensive. He had to be careful with his expenditure. It was very humid and he felt dirty and sticky. He wandered up to Neptuno Street. He turned into San Miguel Street and saw an illuminated sign, too big for the small establishment: 'Bar Okinawa'. It was air-conditioned. Good. He sat at the bar and ate two ham and cheese sandwiches with a Cuban beer. Hatuey. Lighter than English beer, but very good.

He looked around. There was just one couple, drinking cocktails. He finished his beer. When he paid, the barman spoke to him in English:

'Are you looking for entertainment, sir?'

'Hmmm.'

7

'Look at this. If you like one of them, I can call her. They all have telephones. They are quality women.'

The barman gave him a small album. Some of the women were naked; others dressed only in very skimpy underwear. Every photo had a *nom de guerre*: Berta, Olga, Lázara, María, Pucha, Coqui, Azucena, Rosi. They were all white. Two very light mulattas. None were black. GG went through the album a couple of times. He hesitated. The barman sensed that this guy wanted something special. He tried to encourage him.

'There are some very beautiful women here. They always look worse in photos, but in the flesh . . .?'

'No, no thanks.'

'Do you have any preferences? Any particular taste?'

'No.'

'In about half an hour there's an unbelievable porn show starting. It's got everything. For every taste, mister.'

The barman was a bald, middle-aged man, around fifty. Many tourists were gay and came to look for cheap black men with big pricks. He had

8

spent thirty-five years working in bars and he could sum people up. He smiled faintly and added:

'If you've just arrived in Havana, it's best to go to the Shanghai. Warm up the engine gently, mister. It's best to go slowly.'

'What's the Shanghai?'

'A theatre, in the Chinese district. There's a show that starts at ten and goes on till three. I recommend it.'

'Is it far?'

'Far enough. A friend can take you there for a special price. Just for you.'

In fact, the Chinese district is less than a ten-minute walk. The barman rang his taxi-driver friend. They spoke quickly in Spanish. GG did not understand a word. The taxi took him round and round and finally dropped him at the corner of Zanja and Campanario, opposite the theatre. He paid two dollars.

The advertising hoardings were covered with photos of naked men and women, displaying their charms. The awnings had coloured lights. GG crossed over to the pavement in front of the theatre to get a sense of what it was like before going in. There were cheap and dirty prostitutes, food sellers, fried food stalls, people, noise, music, coloured lights. Thousands of Chinese – contaminated by Cubans, they had lost their traditional slow, silent, measured composure. They were shouting, yelling, hawking their wares and moving quickly and incessantly. There was a sickly smell of rotting fruit and fried food from cheap stalls. Two prostitutes approached him smiling. They were sweaty and dirty and smelled bad. One of them had rotting teeth. He hardly looked at them and escaped quickly. He crossed Zanja Street again and bought a ticket. He was charged one dollar fifty cents, more than the real price, and he went into the theatre. He asked if the show had already begun.

'In a minute.'

It was dark and a porn film was showing. Hardly able to see a thing, he sat down in a seat. It looked like an amateur film. The camera shook at times and there were no cuts. And no sound. The actors, a well-endowed man and a fattish, ageing woman with saggy breasts, looked continually at the camera, talked, displayed their sexual organs and carried on fucking a while longer. GG felt a hand squeezing his thigh and heading quickly for his crotch. Frightened, he looked to his right and could not quite make out who it was. It was very dark. He got up nervously, walked along the aisle and stopped at the entrance. He waited there a few minutes. The film finally ended and the lights went up. There were few people in the theatre.

Dozens of people came in and sat down. Just men. Some very young, almost children, twelve or thirteen years old. GG chose a seat in the third row and sat down. Fifteen minutes later the show began with a small orchestra playing a mishmash of rumbas to accompany the action on the stage. A master of ceremonies wearing a blue suit, a red shirt and a yellow and green tie, announced each act with fake seriousness:

'Señoras and señores, ladies and gentlemen, welcome to the most spectacular show on earth. The Great Shanghai Theatre, a Cuban wonder, an all-time wonder of Cuban art, welcomes you most respectfully and guarantees that you will enjoy a non-stop show, without intervals, until three in the morning. Here we never stop, whoever comes! Ha ha! And now, without further ado, here are our stars. A big round of applause for an artiste who has travelled the world, appearing with great success in the Moulin Rouge in Paris, in Rome, New York and other great cities. Recently returned from Mexico after a triumphant tour, we welcome back on stage . . . Madame Vishnú . . . the great showtime jerker . . . The great masturrrrbator!'

Madame Vishnú was almost sixty years old. A bit wrinkly and unpleasant looking. She came on stage dressed as an Arab, covered in veils that she took off throughout her routine. It was simple: she lay several men down on the floor and aroused them with her Arab dance while she stripped completely naked and masturbated each of them. The orchestra played Arab music to a guaracha beat. It was rather boring.

Then a couple came on. Without saying a word, they stripped off in front of the audience and began to fuck straight away on a small platform. They were announced as 'The Reincarnation of the Kamasutra', but they only used three positions. They were followed by a small troupe of six Chinese ballerinas who stripped slowly to the spasmodic rhythm of Chinese Cuban music. When they were completely naked, a black man with an enormous erect prick came on stage and threatened them. They ran away from him, off the stage, screaming in terror. The black man remained on stage and faced the audience, jerking off. In the first row about twenty gays were shouting excitedly. They stood up and screamed at the guy: 'Come on, papi, drench us, the milky rain!'

But the master of ceremonies stepped out and interrupted him. He pushed him off the stage and announced at the top of his voice:

'No milky rain just yet at the Shanghai! The night is young and there are many different surprises to come. We have to wait a bit more.'

The gay men booed him and sat down shouting: 'Envious bitch, miserable fucker, biiitch.'

After a roll of drums and a fanfare of Chinese trumpets, which silenced the queers, the master of ceremonies announced:

'And this is the moment you have all been waiting for, ladies and gentlemen. Brought straight from Africa, for an exclusive appearance in this giant supershow at the Great Shanghai Theatre, we have with us the only man in the world who can come by himself, without anyone touching his gigantic member. An art worthy of the greatest circuses in the world, but we have him here tonight,

13

for your delectation . . . give a big round of applause to our star artist, the supermacho, the great . . . Supermaaan!'

Superman came onto the stage wearing a large gleaming red satin cape. He was a tall, young and slender black man. He stood in the middle of the stage, opened the cape and let it fall to the floor. He was completely naked. Between his legs hung a beast of exaggerated proportions. He was the image of the perfect macho. Complete virility. He seemed to be looking at the audience, but in fact he was focusing on something to his left. Behind the scenes, out of the public view, there were two pretty white boys who started kissing and slowly getting aroused. Superman's hands were stroking his thighs and buttocks. There was total silence in the theatre. They were all staring, hypnotised by that muscular superprick and by the beauty of the young man who sported it. GG looked around and saw that the stalls were completely full. Most were masturbating themselves or their neighbours. Many young men – paid, obviously – were masturbating some older men with their hands or mouths. GG thought that this must be a gay dive. There were no women. He looked back at the stage. Superman had a full erection and was suffering spasms and contractions. GG calculated that the penis must be about sixteen inches long and three inches wide. Exorbitant. Something unimaginable, but true. After a while he realised that Superman had a trick. It looked as if he was just fondling his thighs but in fact he was surreptitiously inserting several fingers up his arse. Suddenly he screwed up his face and came like a bull. He'd gone to the front of the stage. The gays were silently waiting for this stellar moment. They all had their mouths open and their arms outstretched, like a pagan ritual to Priapus. At the precise moment that the first jet of semen shot out, the gays began to shout: 'Divine, divine! Bravo, bravo, divine, bravo!' The orchestra redoubled the drumming and added some climactic notes. The master of ceremonies came onto the stage:

'Five, six, seven! Seven great spurts of milk! Nowhere else in the world! Suuuperman! Milky rain for you all. Anyone with your hands free, applaud. Great applause, please, for this unique artiste. This glory and star of Cuban culture.'

An exhausted but smiling Superman acknowledged the audience, squeezed his tool and directed the last drops at the stalls with the tips of his fingers. He wrapped himself in his cape and left the stage with a display of masculinity and power that sent the respectable public into even greater paroxysms. The euphoria lasted for several minutes longer. The gays who had managed to catch the semen on their faces were smearing and spreading this cream on each other. It was the paroxysm of a phallic festival. Eventually everything quietened down and the master of ceremonies announced the next act, the Stiff Pricks. It was an acrobatic number with four big men and a very skinny young girl. The guys penetrated her at the same time through all her orifices, while maintaining precarious acrobatic poses. Best of all, none of them lost their erection at any moment. GG did not find it very interesting. He began to shift in his seat. He finally made a decision. He got up and headed towards a side aisle. He asked an attendant where the dressing rooms were. The guy said that he could not disturb the artistes. GG put a dollar in his hand. The guy, anxious to be of assistance, asked who he wanted to speak to.

'Superman, of course.'

'Please follow me, sir.'

They went down a dark, dank-smelling corridor. The man knocked on a door and called out:

'Charity! A visitor!'

Someone shouted from inside the room:

'What the fuck is it?'

'There's an admirer here, a foreigner. He wants to say hello to you.'

The door opened. Superman in person looked out. GG held out his hand, smiling, and said:

'I just wanted to congratulate you. I never thought I'd see anything like it. You are a genius.'

Superman was flattered. He was black and as tall as a professional basketball player. He opened the door and invited him in.

'Sit down and wait for me a minute. I'll be ready very soon.'

GG was amazed at what he saw. Superman was dressed as a woman, with an elegant yellow dress, and was applying make-up. He put on a blonde wig. He took the Ochún and Changó amulets that were hanging on a nail on the wall, kissed them and put them around his neck. Finally he applied a few delicate touches of perfume with his fingertips. In front of GG's eyes, he became a beautiful black woman, sensual and alluring. It was only then that he looked at his visitor provocatively and said:

'Are you going to buy me a beer, my little American?'

GG was completely thrown. He didn't know what to say, and stammered:

'Yes.'

'Well, let's go, my angel. The night is ours . . . if you've got what we need.'

'I should say . . . I'm British.'

'All the same to me. It's like you saying you're short-sighted. Let's go.'

They went to a nearby bar, full of prostitutes, sailors and criminals. They had a few beers and were constantly interrupted by people greeting Charity, who was very popular and kept being given drinks. Other people offered them weed, cocaine, opium, at very cheap prices. They did not talk much. GG tried to be courteous and educated – it was the only weapon he had to conquer his rivals. In that environment he felt as defenceless as a newborn baby. He didn't understand a thing, and at the same time he was enjoying it. He and the transvestite had very little to talk about. She came up to him and whispered in his ear.

'Do you like me?'

'Yes.'

'Me, the phallic woman, ha ha.'

GG would have liked to have had an erection, but no. He wanted to be possessed by that black man, that black woman. Charity, Superman – which was it? He wanted to be held and penetrated. He had never felt that desire. At least, never with the same intensity as now.

'Do you want to go to a more private place?'

'Can we go?'

'Of course. Can you pay?'

'Yes.'

Charity took him by the hand and gently led him along Campanario to number 264 Trocadero. The streets were dark, barely lit by the occasional bulb. The Colón district, the big red-light zone of the city. There were small bars open all night on every corner and lights above many doors. Charity had a tiny down-at-heel room in that tenement building on Trocadero.

They went in, and Charity closed the door. The heat was suffocating, humid and sticky. She undressed in two minutes and made him kneel and put it in his mouth. With his knees trembling with emotion, GG touched that enormous animal and began the task that he never imagined could be so pleasurable. Suddenly Charity withdrew and said in an authoritarian, menacing voice:

'I'm a whore! Get that clear!'

'Yes, yes.'

'Pay up. It's twenty dollars.'

GG took out the money and gave it to her.

'Not like that. Leave it on the bed. I like to see the money. Look how it gives me a hard-on.'

Just by looking at the note on the bed, Charity got a full erection.

'You see? I'm a whore. I get worked up when I see money. It excites me. Take your clothes off and turn around.'

GG obeyed. Superman daubed him with Vaseline, put him in position and tried to penetrate him. The pain was so intense that GG screamed loudly.

'Ah ha, just as I thought. You're a little American virgin.'

'No, no, I'm British.'

'It's all the same, my little virgin. Nobody can deal with my prick. You stick it in me, although that baby is very small for my taste.'

They played around like this a bit more. For Charity, a bit of fooling around for half an hour for twenty dollars was a daily routine with these Americans. Stupid white men who can't imagine what life is like and how you have to fight so as not to die of hunger. For GG it was the greatest experience of his life. He never imagined that something so extraordinary could happen to him. When he left, at the door, he tried to kiss Charity. She turned her head. He kissed her on the cheek. Still nervous, he stammered:

'I think . . . I think I love you.'

'You love me? Ha! That's a good one. You're ridiculous, a little shit.'

GG didn't understand those words. His Spanish had a very limited vocabulary, but he loved the black man's sarcastic laugh and his deep voice. He said:

'Thank you for tonight. Can we see each other again?'

'Whenever you want. I am at your disposal, sweetie. You know where my dressing room is . . . this poor unfortunate black lady thinks you're very smart and seductive, ha ha ha.'

And she gave him a kiss, on the forehead.

3

GG went out onto the street and the city seemed different to him.

Had he fallen in love? He walked peacefully along the empty streets. The prostitutes called out to him from every window and door. Since he looked like a weak and defenceless foreigner, he was a perfect target for prostitutes, drug dealers and petty criminals. But he was in such good spirits that he seemed to be floating above the pavement, and he did not hear anything.

He reached the hotel in ten minutes, had a glass of Scotch and went to bed. He dreamed that he was walking in Paris. Sometimes it was Paris and occasionally it turned into Liverpool. Charity was by his side. But he was dressed as a woman and the black man was a powerful guy who kissed and caressed and fondled him in front of everyone. Paris was a pool of water. Or small pools. And they were floating. The black man took his clothes off in front of thousands of people. And there were flowers and people applauded. They walked naked through forests and he had a beautiful penis, well muscled with clearly defined veins and big, swollen, dark balls. The dream changed and became more complex. Suddenly he was a boy and the black man disappeared.

When he woke up it was one in the afternoon. He was tired and still sleepy, but he was also hungry. He decided to take a shower. Feeling refreshed, he went out onto the balcony. He admired the city. It now seemed enchanting. He could learn a bit more Spanish, ask for a bank loan and open up a little shop. He could change his name and forget his past. This was the moment. Everything was possible in this city. Perhaps he could buy an American passport. No, he hated them. A Canadian passport. Perhaps. Another name, another nationality, another life, another profession. In Havana. Why not?

He put on a clean shirt. He went down to the hotel restaurant and had baked red snapper with vegetables for lunch. The prices were low. You could live here with much less money than in

Liverpool. And you could live better. He liked that. While he was waiting to be served, he glanced through a small tourist guide that they had given him in the hotel lobby. He ought to fill in time before the evening. He would try and meet up with Charity again. He felt happy just thinking about that. He considered the tourist attractions that appeared in the guide: excursions, yacht hire for fishing, luxury casinos, theatres – all very expensive for him. At the race track you could place bets starting from a dollar. The races began at four.

He ate slowly. He took a taxi. He went to the racecourse, the Oriental Park. He bet a dollar on each of the first three races. He liked the look of two American horses, from Kentucky – Baby and Sweet Johnny – and a mare from Miami – Big Rose. They all lost. He got into a bad mood. He had always been a bad loser. He went back to the city and headed straight for Sloppy Joe's bar. It was big and pleasant, just a few yards from his hotel. The solid, dark-wood bar, the stools, the relaxed atmosphere were all an invitation to stay and drink. He asked for Scotch, one after another, until he felt slightly drunk. Then he ate a salmon and gherkin sandwich. It was nine o'clock and the anxiety of the wait was killing him. He couldn't stand it any longer, and he asked if he could walk to the Chinese district. The barman gave him directions. In ten minutes he was outside the Shanghai. He thought that he was learning very quickly: 'People in Havana are too crafty. Even the most reliable want to dip their hand in my pocket and come away with a few dollars.'

It was very early. Half past nine. He walked around the theatre and entered by a service door at the back of the building. He already considered himself an expert. He went along a corridor and bumped into a fat old man, who stopped him short:

'What do you want, sir? Where are you going?'

He put a dollar in his hand and said:

'I am a friend of Superman . . . of Charity.'

'Go on in, sir, feel right at home. You can come every night. My name is Alfonso, at your service. If you want something to drink, you just have to call me . . .'

He was a cloying, irritating old man. He left him in mid-sentence and carried on to Superman's dressing room. The door was painted blue and bright red and high up on it someone had stuck cuttings from comics: the name 'Superman' and figures of the hero. In the middle, above the door, were images of the Copper Virgin of Charity and Santa Barbara. Hanging by two nails there was a bunch of tobacco leaves and a little wooden doll in the shape of a man with a big prick and just one leg. The previous evening he hadn't noticed these details. It was a very strange door; everything was very strange there.

He knocked at the door. Nobody replied, but the door was open. He pushed it and went in. He turned on the light and sat down on a chair. Charity would be arriving any time soon. The room was small, hot, dirty and full of all sorts of useless junk. He went over to the small dressing table where Charity put on her make-up, and he thought that she was an anti-artist. Superman went on stage with no make-up and no costume, and played the role of a supermacho. Then he disguised himself as a woman and played another role in his daily life. 'It must be paranoid to live like that, part man, part woman. Or perhaps it's perfect . . . To live in the middle,' he thought. Absent-mindedly he picked up a red lipstick and began applying it, looking at himself in the mirror.

Suddenly Charity came in and interrupted him with a guffaw.

'Oh, sweetie, you don't look good. Don't do it because you look like an old woman from the countryside. Don't try it, my love. I'm the whore here, the Shanghai vedette, the phallic woman, ha ha ha.'

'Good evening.'

'Oh, sweetie, you're so uptight. You can tell you're a virgin.'

'Yes, I wanted to see you and . . .'

'Come here, my sweet. How did you get in? Because I'm the only one with a key. Are you a locksmith or what?'

'The door was open. I only came in a minute ago. And . . . please let me kiss you. I've been desperate to see you.'

'Ayyy, how terrible! What the fuck is this!?'

Superman was looking at the floor. In a corner, under some boxes, was a pool of blood. GG froze.

'They've put a curse on me. Around here there's a lot of envy and people don't like me. They can't stand me being the vedette . . .'

As he spoke, Charity went over to the boxes and threw them aside. He thought that there'd be a decapitated black chicken there, the curse to make his prick go limp and never get up again. That would be the end of Superman. The deadly kryptonite. They'd tried it before. But his own magic was very strong.

'Luckily my protector looks after me like a little girl . . . Ayyy, what's this?'

He pulled away the boxes, utterly horrified. He discovered the body of a man, with his throat cut in a deep gash. The blood had already coagulated. He had a terrible grimace of pain on his face. The blood on the floor was sticky and almost dry. And suddenly one of the stage hands came in, a Chinese dwarf.

'Superman ready? Madame Vishnú didn't come today and you're on in twenty min– Ayyyy, what's that? A dead man! Chinaman knows nothing. A dead man! Ay, what a terrible thing . . ?'

And he ran along the corridor, shouting:

'A dead body with Superman, a dead body with Superman. Police, stop them, police! I know nothing. A dead body with Superman.'

GG and Charity looked at each other in fear. GG suddenly realised that he shouldn't be there and tried to get out quickly along the corridor to the back door. It was Superman's problem, not his. But he ran straight into a tall, big-bellied policeman who was sweating and gasping for breath. GG almost fell over.

'Where are you going, sir? Slow down.'

The policeman grabbed him by the wrist, looked at the corpse and said:

'Aaah, caught red-handed. You're under arrest.'

Half an hour later GG and Charity were giving statements in the police station on Zanja and Escobar. The on-duty officer read out: 'Both suspected of the murder of Mr Thomas Gerhardt, a German citizen, resident in Cuba, foreigner registration number 84522, living at 654 Malecón, second floor, apartment B. The suspects were caught . . .'

Superman was so scared that he was hunched up and silent. But GG, very nervously, insisted a thousand times that he was a British subject and that he was innocent and that they had to let him speak to the British consul. The on-duty officer looked at him, gave a mocking smile and repeated:

'You're caught red-handed and you don't get it. Your heads are already in the noose! Ha!'

He finally agreed to ring the station head at home, because GG kept escalating his threats:

'I'm a world-famous writer. You don't know me because you're illiterate, but this insult will cost you your job. I'll see you begging on the street.'

At that time of night there was just one reporter in the police station. He'd been sitting on a bench, bored and half-asleep, but his ears pricked up. He wrote some notes on his pad, left the station silently and headed for his newspaper office. The following day, there was a front-page statement in the *Havana Post*, the only English-language newspaper in the city: 'Famous British writer in gaol in Havana. Graham Greene a murder suspect.' The offices of AP, UPI, Reuters, France Press and other agencies reproduced the story. A few minutes later, noisy teleprinters sent the news out to newspaper offices and radio stations throughout the world.

4

There is a six-hour time difference between
Havana and the island of Capri, facing Naples.
Graham Greene looked at his watch. Three in the
afternoon. He was alone in the house and was just
waking up after a short one-hour siesta. He loved
living alone. His family, who were much more
sedentary, were now living in the apartments in
Antibes and Paris. He had got up at 7 a.m., as he
always did. He'd had a breakfast of tea, toast and
jam and had spent a long time gazing at the calm
blue sea. He liked to look at the fishermen in their
boats, fishing in the Gulf of Naples, and the small
pleasure yachts and the bustle of people on the
jetty. He could see everything from his house. Now
he'd wait until six, when the white boat would
take the tourists back to Naples. Everything would
go back to normal and he would go to the Piazza
and have a drink at an open-air table. He liked liv-

ing there because everything was quite familiar but nobody bothered him. He assumed that nobody knew who he was – it was perfect for a writer. The only annoying thing was the avalanche of tourists every day, who descended at ten in the morning and then went away at six. Every day, relentlessly, Monday to Sunday. The mayor of Capri liked to repeat that the best form of government was to have as little government as possible. He was delighted by that axiom of freedom that was only applicable to the small island of six thousand inhabitants. In other places it would be difficult or impossible to govern in such a liberal fashion.

A few weeks ago he had finished *The Quiet American* and he still felt tired and confused. He recalled his five-year affair in Saigon with Phuong and how her husband knew about it and tolerated it. They had both been servants in his house. When he came to write, he suppressed that detail and portrayed Phuong as an ordinary, single young woman. The ambitious – or pimp – husband in real life became Phuong's sister in the novel.

He felt guilty. His Christian outlook on life and

his innate decency made him feel continually guilty. Elizabeth, his secretary, had asked him a few days ago, when she was finishing typing up the novel:

'How can you reconcile your faith with hell?'

'I have my ways.'

In fact he could do little to reconcile his good and bad sides. He gazed at the blue sea, sparkling in the sun, and remembered the three-day mini-orgy that he had had in Rome with his American girlfriend Catherine Waltson. He adored Cathy because she had no inhibitions. She was depraved – she didn't know any other way. He had baptised her. At her request, he was her godfather in a Catholic baptism, but they had made love behind the altars of small village churches. Recently, in Rome, she'd decided that she wanted to go to a brothel again. She had dressed up as a man and they went as two male friends out on the town. They did this every so often. She was wilful and they had enjoyed a mad, sado-masochistic relationship for some years. Catherine's husband, an English lord much older than her, was a boring, passive man. She was young, slender, attractive and she did not know what to do with so much time, money and energy.

GG presumed that the same thing happened to all slightly virile writers: bored women who had read their books appeared everywhere, became fascinated and set out to ensnare the writers and have a bit of fun. It was the reason he holed up in Capri as often as he could, and changed his telephone number every few months. Frivolous, superficial people bothered him. And the older he got, the more frivolous, superficial people seemed to surround him. Or was it him – was he getting boring, losing his lightness and his sense of humour?

'The important thing is moderation. Avoid excesses. The three-day orgy in Rome was perfect. A week would have been tiresome and tedious. You must always leave a bit of desire in reserve,' GG thought. He went over to the record player and put on Mozart's *Serenata Notturna*. He sat in his favourite armchair and listened with his eyes closed. He thought about his secretary's question again and answered it to himself: 'Balance, my dear Elizabeth. A bit of hell and a bit of paradise. It's a simple formula. And it works.'

Two days earlier he had quickly dispatched a French journalist from *Lire* magazine. He had arrived at ten in the morning and had tried to stay all day and ask personal questions. GG was fifty-one, but there were times he felt much older. He had lived a fast, intense life, with his foot on the accelerator all the time. Every day he felt more emotionally drained and exhausted. He went over to his desk and picked up the manuscript of *The Quiet American* again. He had marked a few slightly philosophical passages and he wanted to go over them again. He had to whittle away, so that these paragraphs just contained the essence, one or two lines. 'Philosophy in novels is like bitter in cocktails. Two drops. Three is too many'.

He smiled when he remembered the journalist's look of disgust when he told him: 'I write out of necessity. A book is like a boil that has to be lanced when it is fully formed. A book is as epidermal as an abscess.' The journalist was clearly well-mannered and formal, as critics of art and literature tend to be. Too clean and ordered and boring. They are terrified by disorder, dirt and the unexpected. They are scared of what might escape them. What is incomprehensible. What they cannot label and classify.

He put aside the manuscript of the novel and

picked up *The Daily Telegraph*. He read the headlines on the first page, and then gave up. He shut
his eyes again and paid attention to the Mozart. He
needed to recover his mental coherence, his normal aplomb.

He felt uneasy, anxious, troubled, slightly bitter,
sad and lonely. This always happened to him
when he finished a book. He called it convales-
cence. He drew all his characters from reality,
although, to avoid subsequent complaints, he
repeated insistently that they came from his imag-
ination. He always felt guilty and treacherous
every time he finished a novel. He continued
drowsily listening to Mozart. The phone ringing
woke him up. It was his editor from Panther Books
in London.

'Graham?'

'Yes?'

'I just wanted to check that you were there and
that all's well.'

'Are you looking after me or controlling me?'

'The BBC has just put out a news item. I think
it's a tasteless joke.'

'What does it say?'

'That you spent the night in a cell in Havana.

You are a suspect for the murder of a German. And, even worse: there is another suspect. A porn artiste with a dubious reputation, a friend of yours. It seems that you were together when the crime took place.'

'It's a mistake.'

'So I see.'

'I don't understand how ...'

'There is nothing to understand, Graham. We'll just have to wait, patiently. I'll keep you informed.'

'Many thanks. Goodbye.'

GG felt increasingly uneasy. He went to the doorway and looked out at the sea. Perhaps he should call the British Embassy in Havana, ask for information and say that he was living peacefully in Capri, and demand an official statement clarifying this mistaken and unpleasant situation.

The phone rang again. It was the deputy director of press and publicity at Panther Books.

'Hello, Mr Greene. I know what's happened. I've just been talking to the editor-in-chief and I've had an idea. May I ask you something?'

'Go ahead.'

'Please don't do anything. Have you called Havana?'

'No, I'll do it as soon as we get off the phone.'

'No, please don't. Quite the reverse. Disappear. Don't answer the telephone. Go off incognito to some small Italian village. Somewhere without a phone.'

'I don't understand.'

'The idea is that you really are in Havana, mixed up in this ugly affair.'

'Impossible. Are you mad?'

'Your book sales will shoot up. I'll take care of everything.'

'I have my principles. I can't ...'

'I'm sorry. I'm not asking you to do anything to tarnish those principles, Mr Greene. I just want you to disappear, so that no journalist can find you. We want to launch an urgent publicity campaign. Right this minute. Inside a week we'll have a press conference for you here and we'll explain that it has all been an unfortunate mistake.'

'That makes no sense.'

'It makes commercial sense. I'm working for you. And that's a pleasure for me because I adore your books and ...'

'Please, please!'

'All right. Let me explain. I'm writing a press

release. I am saying that Panther Books is employing the best criminal lawyer in London to travel immediately to Havana and organise your defence. And that we will also ask Scotland Yard to send one of their best detectives to Havana since we are sure that you are innocent. What do you think?'

'Ohhh, but ...'

'It's thrilling, Mr Greene. I am really enjoying this emergency campaign. Please, just disappear, very quietly. Get out of Capri as soon as possible. And keep in contact with me. You must ring me every day. I'll keep your whereabouts secret.'

GG thought about it for a few seconds and let out a loud sigh.

'Fine. You can count on me.'

'Perfect. We'll have a champagne celebration. Goodbye, Mr Greene.'

5

At five-thirty in the afternoon, GG carefully closed all the doors and windows in his house. He took a small bag with some personal effects and a carbon copy of the manuscript of *The Quiet American*. He adjusted his panama hat and sunglasses. He closed the front door carefully, double-locked it and set off down the hill to the jetty. He enjoyed smelling the delicate scent of the flowers in the gardens along the narrow road. He boarded the boat just in time.

An hour later, at seven in the evening, he got off in the docks in Naples. He was now feeling much better. Inactivity made him anxious and made him think stupid thoughts. When he travelled, he regained his self-confidence, and put to one side all those questions that could not be resolved: guilt, fear of old age and loneliness, that sense of being crushed by routine and daily monotony. On board he had drunk a couple of glasses of brandy. So everything was fine. Onwards.

He headed for the railway station. The night train to Rome was leaving at nine, and he reserved a couchette. He had a light dinner at a nearby trattoria and at nine on the dot he was on his way. He was in Rome at six a.m. on Monday. He had slept little and badly. It always happened – the jolting of the train prevented him from sleeping. He went to the airport and checked the best way of getting to New York, Chicago or Miami. The only possible combination was to leave an hour later for Paris, wait there for four hours and then take a Super G Constellation – a very modern plane, a four-engined turboprop – that would get him across the Atlantic, to New York, in only eleven hours. From New York, he caught a connection to Miami and he finally landed in Havana on Tuesday 19 July at three in the afternoon. He did the arithmetic. A total of thirty-seven hours since he had left his house in Capri.

When he got off the plane, he was hit by the heat, the humidity and the smell of wet earth and rotten fruit. Capri, the Mediterranean in general, was much more pleasant. The climate and the smells were more delicate. This was excessive, beyond the normal limits.

When he stepped out of the airport, a smiling mulatto almost forced him to get into his new taxi: a 1948 Buick, playing the latest hit song on the CMQ station: 'Domitila, where you go? With that shawl from Manila, where you go?'

'Are you from the United States, sir?'

'I'm British.'

'Ah well, if you are looking for a hotel, I can take you to the Inglaterra.'

'Is it a good hotel?'

'Excellent. I recommend it.'

They set off. GG needed a comfortable bed, darkness, silence and peace. He needed to sleep for a few hours and recover. Lack of sleep had given him a headache. He had come to the Caribbean before and it always took him a couple of days to adapt to the noise, the light, the food, the people, the heat and the humidity. His family had close links to the Caribbean, going back in time. To the island of Saint Kitts specifically. When his grandfather was fifteen, he had been sent to Saint Kitts to join his brother and help him run the family sugar-cane plantation. A few months later his brother had died of yellow fever. He was only nineteen and he left thirteen children behind. Some time later, GG's grandfather had returned to the family house in Bedfordshire, but he could never forget the small Caribbean island. Finally, when he was an old man, he left his wife and children and went back and died there. Some years earlier GG had visited the cemetery, the two graves next to each other, and he had prayed for the souls of the two brothers in the chapel that resembled an English parish church. He too was attracted to the Caribbean and to Central America.

At the hotel reception, nothing happened. There were three members of staff, who each covered an eight-hour shift. The one on duty was perhaps less cultured. He did not react to GG's name.

'We have an excellent suite available, sir, if you would like . . .'

'No, thank you. I just need a single room, as long as it's comfortable, clean and well ventilated.'

'Overlooking the street, Central Park?'

'Yes.'

The bellboy took him to a room on the second floor. When he was on his own, he put his few personal effects on the chest of drawers. The paper-

43

back of *Creatures of Circumstances* by W. Somerset Maugham caught his eye again. A collection of short stories. They didn't get on. They could not stand one another, but each read the other's work, in secret. GG admired the light touch and grace of Maugham's plots and hated his frivolity, and Maugham was fascinated by the psychological perfection of GG's characters, but was put off by his complicated plots, which seemed to mesh like clockwork.

GG had no intention of giving him any free publicity. Best to ignore him. So he hid the book away in his bag and threw it in a drawer. Nobody should see it, not even the maid. In any event, he would not read the book to the end. He had read so much in his life that he was now excessively selective. He could not even read his own books again once they were published. He'd completely forgotten some of them. He preferred reading newspapers and magazines. He had a very cold shower, took an aspirin with a glass of water, closed the curtains, turned on the air-conditioning and went to bed to recover. He had not the faintest idea what he would do in Havana. He had decided on this trip without thinking about it. Sometimes he felt that he spent his life running away from himself. Always running away, from wherever he was.

He slept very little. Someone knocking at the door woke him up. He got up, feeling giddy. He opened the door. There were two policemen dressed in blue and a fat, pot-bellied man dressed in a white drill suit, two-tone shoes – black and white – and a narrow, ridiculous, multicoloured floral tie. The three were sweating copiously and looked severe. They were clearly ready to make an arrest. Only the fat man with the tie spoke, after flashing his badge:

'Mr Graham Greene?'

'Yes.'

'Do you understand Spanish?'

'Yes.'

'Get dressed and come with us.'

'Could you tell me . . .'

'You'll know soon enough.'

They came into the room, turned on the light and stood by the door. GG went to the bathroom. He washed his face and got dressed. He knew that it was pointless to ask for explanations in these cases. When he was ready, the fat man spoke again:

'Remember to bring your passport and any other form of identity. From now you are under arrest, in the custody of the Military Intelligence Service of the Republic of Cuba.'

6

GG looked at his watch. Six-thirty in the evening. He had slept scarcely two hours. He was in a small office, in a building that he presumed housed the Intelligence Service, the SIM. He did not know what was happening, and decided to wait quietly. The fat man was standing by the desk. The two policemen were mounting guard outside. The fat man invited him to sit on a sofa and asked:

'Well then, Mr Greene, what have you got to tell us?'

'I've got nothing to say. You need to tell me what I am doing here and why you are bothering me.'

'Have you read today's *New York Times*?'

'It hasn't crossed my mind. I'm dead tired.'

'Read it.'

He pointed to an article in the international news section. They had reproduced the press release from Panther Books. The publishers stated that they had hired the best criminal lawyer in London, and that two Scotland Yard detectives would be travelling to Havana to help the authorities clarify the situation. They insisted that GG was innocent of the murder and declared that this was a 'scandalous and unexpected situation that is perplexing all of GG's friends'. A small masterpiece designed to create uncertainty and attract attention. The piece ended with an announcement that, despite everything, the bookshops would soon receive delivery of 'one of the best novels written by GG, set in Indo-China'. And it mentioned some recent titles, published by Panther Books: *The Confidential Agent, The Power and the Glory, The End of the Affair,* etc.

GG thought for a moment after reading this and said:

'My editor hasn't consulted me about . . .'

'Don't worry. We already know that another man has been passing himself off as you. We know that you arrived today, at Boyeros, on a flight from Miami, at three in the afternoon. And we also know that the other man is staying at the Hotel Inglaterra, like you. We are always very well informed, Mr Greene.'

GG thought that the information he had was rather stupid and irrelevant, but he kept quiet. The fat man was sly and looked like a real brute, very different to a professional intelligence officer. The fat man said to him:

'OK. I'm going to introduce you to someone who is very interested in meeting you, Mr Greene.'

He opened the door and called someone who was waiting outside. A tall, middle-aged man in a well-cut but rather plain suit came in. He held out his hand, with a polite smile, and introduced himself. He also showed an official identity card:

'Robert Tripp, FBI special agent.'

'Pleased to meet you.'

'Let's not waste time. We know about everything. We wanted to talk to you in a place that was discreet.'

'And unpleasant.'

'That's not important. Your visit to Havana has surprised us. That is why I would ask you to be as discreet as possible. Keep on the sidelines, I mean.'

'I shouldn't meddle, you mean.'

'The murder of this German is much more complicated than you might think, Mr Greene. We need time to investigate.'

'Who was the dead man?'

'Can I have your word of honour not to speak about this?'

'Of course.'

'His real name was Rudolph Schreiber. A submarine dropped him on the coast of Yucatán on October 1945, near a beach called Progreso. Four days later he entered Havana under the false name of Thomas Gerhardt, on a ferry from New Orleans. The guy got ahead quickly. He was a professional. His passport had stamps dating from 1934 from Buenos Aires, Bogotá, Quito, Río de Janeiro and Caracas. He passed himself off as a vacuum-cleaner salesman and he created a very credible story for himself as being a liberal, apolitical, drifting adventurer, who had left Argentina when Nazism began to turn the screws. In reality he was a high-ranking SS officer in Berlin, and was the commandant of Buchenwald concentration camp for two years. In Havana he opened a vacuum-cleaner shop and rented an apartment with a sea view at the top of a building on the Malecón. Well, we've had him under observation for ten years. We know that he is – was – a professional. He could have contacts here and in other countries. No use. We couldn't prove anything. We had everything lined up to detain him, take him in secret to Washington and try him as a war criminal. We had decided that we'd conduct the operation next week, with the utmost discretion. We hadn't even informed the Cuban authorities yet. There were only three of us who knew the details of the operation. What's happened? It might be very serious. Perhaps, though I'd say definitely, we have a mole in our central office. Do you understand the seriousness of the situation?'

'And why are you telling me all this if it is so delicate?'

'Because we have asked for the collaboration of the British Secret Service. This case is a lot bigger and more complex than you might imagine.'

'And more complex than what you've told me.'

'Of course. I've only told you a very small part of the whole affair.'

'That makes sense, and thank you. I don't want to know secret information and then become a target.'

'The intelligence services of your country have asked us to protect you because your life might be in danger while you are in Havana.'

'And?'

'Here we can do very little or nothing. It's better that you know the situation, at least the part that affects you personally. You're the best person to watch your own back.'

'Do you have any specific advice?'

'This is a chaotic and sinful city, Mr Greene. Very sinful. A city that burns in the devil's flames. I repeat that we can do very little to protect you. In practice, we can do nothing. I suggest that you return to Europe today. That would be best.'

'No, Mr Tripp, I'd rather spend a few days here. I have had a terrible thirty-seven-hour journey. I'm dead tired. I don't understand anything that is going on, and you're asking me to forget it all and go home.'

'That's just my advice. For your security.'

'Thanks, but no. Let's do something else.'

'What?'

'First and foremost, I need my stay here to be a secret. No one must know. And I'd also very much like to meet the person who is masquerading as me and ask him a couple of questions.'

'I now see why MI5 and MI6 hold you in such high regard. They were quite insistent that we should look after you.'

'I didn't know that I was so appreciated.'

Robert Tripp gave a conspiratorial smile and said:

'Don't worry about keeping things secret. Here the journalists run around like children, after the money. But they aren't very professional and they don't create problems for anyone. With regard to your second request, we'll have to see. I also need to find the porn star and the other man. They've disappeared.'

'What? Aren't they under arrest?'

'No, they were released through lack of evidence. At least, that is the official explanation. There were some prints at the scene of the crime that did not match the suspects' prints.'

'Just that?'

'Ummm.'

'Very strange. I don't think that the police here are such innocents.'

'I don't either. But here the saying goes that the monkey dances for money. They were released on bail and they should be traceable, but they've disappeared.'

GG felt very tired and he was thinking sluggishly.

He was confused, and felt he'd had enough for one day. But, despite his exhaustion, he thought that he could kill two birds with one stone: everyone was asking him to remain hidden and he liked being hidden, so that's what he would do. And it would be very good to increase his book sales over a few days. 'Also, I'm getting some ideas for a new novel here. After all, Capri is very boring. Europe is getting more tedious by the day. It wasn't like that before the war. There was less money and more life.'

'If you will allow me a suggestion, Mr Greene: change hotels and move to a more anonymous one. The Bristol, for example. It is more basic than the Inglaterra, but nobody would notice you. In the Inglaterra you are too exposed.'

They left the SIM building. Fortunately the unpleasant fat man had disappeared. The FBI agent had a Cadillac, with air-conditioning, tinted windows, diplomatic plates and a chauffeur. They went straight to the Hotel Bristol, on Amistad and San Rafael. Three blocks from the Inglaterra. They had availability. He registered. Tripp suggested that they had dinner together and he waited while he went back to the Inglaterra to collect his things.

'I am very tired, Mr Tripp, but I'm hungry. So it would be a pleasure to have dinner with you.'

'Would you prefer international or Chinese cuisine?'

'I haven't eaten Chinese for a long time.'

'We'll go to the Chinese district.'

They got out of the Cadillac on Zanja and Campanario, opposite the Shanghai. They went over to look at the posters. Superman was not on the programme, so they asked after him at the box office.

'Superman hasn't worked here for days, sir. That's all I know.'

They went to the Fo Luong which had delicious food, air-conditioning and two beautiful petite waitresses. GG liked them a lot. 'They are not exactly Chinese, but they are also not exactly black,' he remarked.

'In Cuba nothing is exact. That's the appeal of the place.'

'Ohhh.'

'They're sisters, Mr Greene. Their father owns this restaurant. He's pure Chinese. And their mother is a very beautiful black woman. The result is very attractive.'

'You're not wasting your time in Havana. You know everything.'

'I come here often. For work.'

'They are more beautiful than Thai women. How can that be?'

'Don't think too much about them because they're not available. In Havana there are thousands like those two. A beautiful mixture. Chinese and black. But they have a very rigid, closed, family education. There's no way around it, no point in hoping.'

'There must be the occasional one in the brothels?'

'No, in the brothels you can find everything – even French and Italian women. But you'll never find a Chinese mulatta.'

After dinner, they strolled along the street for a few minutes. The Cadillac was waiting for them on Zanja, a couple of blocks away. It wasn't attracting attention. Havana had eight hundred thousand inhabitants and some six hundred thousand cars.

'I would like you to accompany me to the Hotel Inglaterra, Mr Greene. I want to search the room that your double occupied. The Cuban police have it sealed off. You might be interested.'

'I'll make a superhuman effort. I haven't slept for two days.'

'It'll be worthwhile.'

They went to the hotel. Mr Tripp showed a SIM card and asked to have room 305 opened for a search. They went up in the lift. On the way up, GG asked:

'Do you have a Cuban intelligence service card?'

'We work closely together.'

'But none of them have an FBI card.'

Robert Tripp did not answer. They went into the room, accompanied by the bellboy, who waited silently by the door. He faced the corridor discreetly. He didn't want to see anything. He was black, and blacks had enough problems already without going looking for them. It was better for him not to see anything. GG walked up and down, watching, but with his hands behind his back. He knew that he couldn't touch anything. Tripp went through the drawers carefully. Nothing there. In the wardrobe he found a small bag, a shirt and some dirty socks. At the back there was an album of beautiful old pornographic photos. They were for sale close by, on the stalls in Neptuno Street.

There was also a wallet with a British passport in the name of George Greene, a journalist, a Liverpool resident. Tripp took everything and they went down to reception. They showed the photo to the man on the desk.

'Yes, that's him. I asked for an autograph and he signed this book.'

He showed him the first page of the novel.

'But the name in this passport is George, not Graham, so what happened?'

'I think that it was me who got confused. I'd been reading this novel a minute earlier and the gentleman arrived looking for a room. I asked him his name and he said: "Mr Greene, British." I got excited. I thought that he was the writer. I took his passport but I gave it back to him without looking at it. I immediately asked for his autograph and offered him a bottle of Scotch, on the house.'

'And what did he do?'

'He accepted. Now I remember that he looked confused.'

'Confused, but he accepted the whisky, he signed the book and he passed himself off as someone else.'

'Well, if you put it like that.'

Tripp took the young man's particulars and told him that he might have to make a formal statement to the police. He tipped the bellboy a few coins and they went out onto the pavement.

'Very well, Mr Greene, at least we know that he is not a professional. He's on the run without identification and perhaps without any money. It seems that it all happened by chance, and that he took advantage of the situation to have some free whisky and to feel famous and important. Now he's running scared, like a rat in a sewer. And that's where I'll have to look for him. In the sewers.'

'One more idiot in this vale of tears.'

'In any event, I need to apprehend him. Early tomorrow I'll ask the Cuban authorities to help.'

'I'm going to bed. Please don't wake me up tomorrow. My brain can't take any more.'

'Have a good rest, Mr Greene.'

7

The next day, GG woke up at an unusual time: ten-thirty in the morning. He opened the curtains. The view was a dirty wall a yard away. He preferred the curtains. He picked up the phone and asked for a continental breakfast.

'We don't have room service, sir. I'm sorry.'

He went down to the restaurant. It had shut at ten. It would open again for lunch, from 12 to 3 p.m. 'The drawbacks of staying in a third-class hotel,' he thought calmly. He was an experienced traveller. He knew that it would take him two or three days to work out how the city operated on a basic level. He went in search of a decent café. Near by, on the corner of San Rafael and Galiano, there were large shops several storeys high. They all had cafés on the ground floor. He had breakfast in El Encanto. It was still early and there weren't many people wandering around the store. While he drank his coffee with milk, he glanced at a Cuban newspaper that he had bought on the corner. With the journey he had completely lost track of the date. It was Wednesday 20 July 1955. The front-page headlines focused on Cuban gossip, which did not greatly interest him. He put the paper to one side without opening it.

A man sat down beside him. He put an envelope on the counter, by his cup, looked him in the eyes and said in a friendly fashion:

'Read it, please.'

GG took the envelope and opened it. The man got up from the stool.

'Goodbye then,' he said. 'I hope that we'll meet up.'

It was a typewritten note:

We invite you to meet us tonight at 8 p.m.
at the main entrance to Coney Island Park.
Don't say anything to the police or the FBI.
You will find it very interesting. Burn this
message.

GG put it in his jacket pocket. Why burn it? He paid and walked around. He bought a white shirt and a white guayabera. Very cool. That would be enough for a few days. The hotel had a laundry service. After walking for an hour, he felt exhausted. The heat and humidity in July are unbearable. He went back to his room and took refuge once more in the air-conditioning. He picked up the manuscript of *The Quiet American*. It was always the same. When he had a book ready to be sent to the publishers, he couldn't let it go. He revised it time and again. And he found little details that he corrected continually. He read: 'From childhood I had never believed in permanence and yet I had longed for it. Always I was afraid of losing happiness. This month, next year, Phuong would leave me. If not next year, in three years. Death was the only absolute value in my world.'

He remembered when Phuong would sleep next to him some nights. Did Phuong love both of them? Her husband and him? Or neither of them? The novel would have turned out much better if he had dared to tell the real, harsh truth. It had been a triangle. Days of love, sex, dreaming, disillusionment, hope. He often wished that Phuong's husband would leave once and for all. But this didn't happen. The man preferred to lend him his wife for a few hours every day, and calmly accept payment for his work as a gardener-errand boy-butler-servant, all the time turning a blind eye. He always treated GG with excessive respect. The perfect subordinate. That way he kept his distance and it seemed that he knew nothing. But he knew everything. It is impossible to keep a secret like that for five years. Many nights, Phuong stayed with him, prepared him two or three pipes of opium, and they made love gently and then slept unconcerned until the following morning. What did Phuong's husband do during those nights? GG tried to put out of his mind the idea that he used both of them for money.

On several occasions Phuong had assured him that she loved him, and that she was prepared to leave Saigon and go with him. Was that true? The end was painful. Five years with one woman is a long time. Too long. And from then on he'd had Catherine Waltson in his life. But Cathy was just a fling, a diversion, and nothing more. Phuong was a delicate little bird. A woman that one could love gently. She was innocent and at the same time she applied Buddhist philosophy with complete naturalness: 'I, here, now.' That made her invulnerable. Christian philosophy is too imperfect. It has been manipulated and twisted *ad nauseam* and now its only purpose is to make its followers feel remorseful.

When they made love, GG thought that Phuong twittered with pleasure. She sang softly. Not excessively, without raising her voice. But money ruined everything and created doubt: did she love him or did she just need his money? Sometimes he felt that he was paying a personal whore and her pimp. And that was all.

Finally, when he decided to write the novel, he had been out of Saigon for a year. That is, he'd got his distance. He could see everything more clearly. He decided to write Phuong as an enchanting but pragmatic woman, someone who loved peace and security. Not romantic. He also decided to remove the constant, unsettling presence of her husband in the house. He didn't want to write a complex psychological novel, with twists and lurid entanglements. It would be very difficult to write and to read. He preferred to do something more simple. Reality is always too complicated – that's why it's ungraspable. Literature can only be a simplified truth, a half-truth. It cannot be pretentious. It cannot aspire to anything more. On page eighty of the novel, he had reflected briefly on this point. He had corrected it until the idea became just a tangential interruption in the text. Scarcely a superficial wound on the body of the book:

> Wouldn't we all do better not trying to understand, accepting the fact that no human being will ever understand another, not a wife a husband, a lover a mistress, nor a parent a child. Perhaps that's why men have invented God – a being capable of understanding. Perhaps if I wanted to be understood or to understand I would bamboozle myself into belief, but I am a reporter; God exists only for leader-writers.

GG went through all the reflections that he had put in the book. A novel is like a building. You can't place doors and windows just anywhere. You have to know exactly where they go. And the size, the style and the colour that they will be. Like buildings, some novels are exceptionally good, they last, and millions of people visit them. Others are anodyne and vulgar, they attract no one and they collapse with the passing of time. Only mad spirits, daring people, agitators, take the risk of building lasting, moving novels that will disturb and shake their visitors. Madness is decisive.

Further on he reread a paragraph that really pleased him:

I know how cruel and bad my temper can be. Now I think it's a little better – the East has done that for me – not sweeter, but quieter. Perhaps it's simply that I'm five years older.

He smiled, very satisfied. It was perfect. Impossible to improve it. It was a wink to the intelligent reader. He sometimes liked to reveal himself like this, let something of himself show to readers who knew his earlier books. There were ideas that were repeated here and there.

He had lunch at two, had a long, undisturbed siesta and listened to the radio in his room for a while. He wanted to get used to listening to Spanish. He felt that something interesting might happen in the evening, although he couldn't imagine what it might be. At six he went looking for a bar. The hour for libations. There were a lot of bars, one on every corner. It was the centre of the city, the commercial area. It was a hive of activity, buzzing with traffic and noise. Around seven the shops started closing and the streets became quieter. Cubans had adopted American timetables and habits: they got up early, by eight everything was already running, and between six and seven in the evening, the city began to flag. Lunch at midday, dinner at eight. It was a beautiful city, but at the same time it breathed pragmatism, efficiency and competitiveness. The United States as a neighbour was too powerful, too influential and too close. This closeness had, like everything, advantages and disadvantages. You could make two equally long lists, for and against.

GG drank a gin and tonic while he listened to the quick-fire, sloppy, unintelligible Spanish being spoken around him. Cuba is the worst place in the world to learn Spanish. When Cubans speak, they express how they are: happy, impulsive and careless and, in most cases, naïve and chaotic.

At half past seven he found a taxi that took him along the Malecón, going west. They carried on down Quinta Avenida. At ten to eight they reached the main entrance to Coney Island. There were a lot of people, music, noise and movement. It was a giant amusement park. Opposite, on the other side of the main road, there were a number of small bars, all kinds of stalls, street musicians, prostitutes. He liked the feel of the place. Someone came up to him smiling, and put an arm around his shoulders in familiar fashion. It was the guy who had given him the envelope in the café. He greeted him as if they were lifelong friends, with a broad smile.

'Graham, how are you? Let's go, it's close by.'

He was wearing a light suit and a tie. He positioned himself on GG's left-hand side and gently led him into the amusement park, where they mingled with the crowds. On his right was another man, also well dressed. They went round and round and stopped in front of several stalls. GG realised that they were taking their time to do a double-check, in case anyone was following them.

GG let them do this, but he was getting nervous. He pursed his lips, in a worried fashion. No – he smiled faintly – they shouldn't see that he was anxious and afraid. They were professionals and knew what they were doing. At least, that is how it seemed.

They went to the Tunnel of Love at the far end of the park. They handed tickets to the man on the door and went in, but they didn't get into a carriage. They walked along the platform, went into the tunnel and waited for a moment at the first bend. The man who had collected the tickets followed them and, without saying a word, opened a small hatch. They went out through it. They were in the open air again. The tall grass and the large façade of the tunnel shielded them from prying eyes. GG looked at his watch: eight-twenty. It was slowly getting dark. There was still a lot of light. At nine the sun would be completely hidden. They walked towards the back fence. Two other guys were waiting for them. One was wearing a white, impeccable guayabera. The other had on a simple short-sleeved shirt. The one with the guayabera had a lilting voice and directed everything with military precision.

'Is she inside?' he asked the men accompanying GG.

'Yes.'

'And the maid left?'

'Half an hour ago.'

'Is she alone?'

'Yes.'

'Let's go.'

The man in the shirt had some wire cutters in a carpenter's bag, along with other tools. He snipped the fence and pulled it up a bit. They went through the fence and found themselves in the patio of a two-storey mansion. It was a beautiful neo-classical stone building, with elegant stained-glass windows. Two German shepherd dogs came quickly across to them. They seemed like attack wolves. The one with the shirt took some pieces of meat out of his pocket and threw them. The dogs didn't see the meat. They were going to attack. The one with the guayabera already had a gun with a silencer in his hand. He killed them with two shots. It was very quick and he had a perfect aim. He put the bullets into the animals' brains. They didn't even have time to yelp. They fell to the floor dead.

They moved quickly to the back door. It was open. Someone had left it slightly ajar. They went in. They all had guns with silencers, and they parted company stealthily. The one with the white guayabera went up the stairs. The others searched the rooms on the ground floor.

The leader came down a few minutes later and asked:

'Anyone else here?'

'No.'

'Come up.'

They took GG with them. The leader said, courteously:

'You first, please.'

They entered a bedroom on the top floor. A blonde, very white woman, around fifty, was tied to a chair. She had strips of tape over her mouth and she looked at them terrified. The one with the white guayabera said to her:

'I'm going to take the gag off. Don't try to shout because nobody will hear you and it will be a waste of time. And I don't want to have to listen to you shouting.'

The guy was cold and efficient. He tore off the gag. The woman spoke Spanish with a strong accent.

'Please, show some pity.'

'Did you show pity? How many Jews did you kill?'

'None, I am innocent. I don't have blood on my hands.'

'Don't be stupid and don't lie. We know your entire story.'

'I can tell you who the other Nazis in Havana are. If you let me go . . .'

'We have a complete list of the Nazis living in Havana and throughout Latin America. Well, I won't exaggerate: the list is almost complete. And we are beginning to execute them. You are the second person. There is no appeal. An eye for an eye and a tooth for a tooth.'

The woman closed her eyes tightly because the guy in the guayabera raised his gun quickly, positioned it a few inches from her temple and fired. The head shuddered and slumped. The dull thud of the bullet. A small stain of blood spread across the woman's neck and trickled onto her lace night-gown. The bullet did not come out of the other side of the head. It was lodged in the brain. The man looked at his guayabera carefully. There were no spatters. He moved away a few paces and studied his work closely. He gave a reflex nod of approval, as if he were contemplating a recently finished sculpture. He put away his gun and spoke to the other three:

'Look through the stuff while I speak to our special guest, ha ha ha. Are you nervous, Mr Greene?'

'No.'

'Have you ever killed?'

'No.'

'It's very easy. Would you like to learn? A writer must know a bit about everything.'

GG kept quiet. He was not interested in exchanging stupid remarks with this person while there was a corpse bleeding a few feet away from him. The blood was now gushing out. Pints and yet more pints of blood. GG calculated that it would take a few minutes to coagulate and seal over the hole. He tried to look somewhere else, but his eyes kept returning to this small hole where the liquid was flowing out. His mind was suddenly bombarded with the many deaths that he had seen during the war in Indo-China. They were mainly decaying and putrefying bodies. He had never seen anyone killed before. It seemed rather simple. Destroying is always easy.

The guy smiled at him sardonically and waited. He knew that GG was affected. A writer is never a man of action. The guy knew that he was upsetting him and he was enjoying it. He repeated the question:

'Would you like to learn, Mr Greene? I can give you a couple of lessons. Free.'

'I didn't come here to talk rubbish.'

'You have no idea why we have invited you, sir. Let me first introduce myself. I am the Captain. And my group is called Habash. It is much bigger than this commando unit that you see in action. Habash is everywhere.'

'And what is my part in all this?'

'We had not anticipated that a famous writer would appear in the dressing room of such a vulgar porn artist. I must admit that this was an error in our calculations. We wanted to draw the attention of the press to this execution. And we thought that it was good to do something scandalous. But the Cuban press completely ignores what happens in those filthy neighbourhoods. For them, only the government and high society are important.'

'But it wasn't me who was there.'

'It was published in *The Havana Post.*'

'It's a mistake.'

'No more mistakes. Pay attention because I'm going to tell you something that will interest you: we're going to execute the Nazis who fled. They are war criminals. It has been a slow task, but not one will escape. It doesn't matter where they hide. Habash has a very long reach. Habash spans the whole world, and there will be no mercy. We think that you can help us. I want them to suffer while they are waiting for us. I want them to shit themselves with fear.'

'Can you be a bit more specific?'

'Write an article, a book, whatever. We will give you all the information that you need. We have been working for ten years. Meticulously.'

'Errr . . .'

'Think about it. I trust that you will know how to protect your sources, that you'll know very well what you'll have to keep to yourself.'

'Of course.'

'We will be back in contact with you. Remember that there are many of us. It is very easy for us to keep you under observation. Don't interpret this as a threat, but we are very cautious.'

During this time, the other three had moved a large wardrobe aside and had found a safe built into the wall. They worked carefully until they opened it. GG looked at them several times out of the corner of his eye. They emptied the safe. They filled two bags with jewellery and money. They closed the safe and put the wardrobe back in its place. They really were very meticulous. And they acted coldly. 'These people are very dangerous,' he thought.

A few minutes later they left him in the Tunnel of Love and disappeared. GG felt dazed in the midst of the crowd. He liked to think that he was a hard man, but in truth he had not yet recovered. He looked at his watch. Eight fifty-five in the evening. It was all so quick. He headed towards the main entrance, crossed Quinta Avenida and stopped at one of the bars. He went into the small, dark and dingy bar that smelt of fried food and urine. He went up to the counter and asked for a whisky.

'I've only got rum, aguardiente and cold beer.'

'Give me a rum.'

He was served a measure, he gulped it down in one and asked for another. Only a few people at the tables. In one corner a black man was messing around: he was tapping bottles and tins, blowing a whistle, contorting his mouth and making all kinds of noises, imitating trumpets and conga drums. At first GG thought he was a madman or an imbecile. After the second shot of rum, he paid closer attention. The guy knew what he was doing, and liked to do it his way. The barman came across to talk to him. There weren't many customers.

'That's El Chori. He's been playing here for years.'

'Is that right?'

'And important people come to see him. He's an international artiste.'

'Ahhh.'

The barman shouted:

'Chori, sing something so that the gentleman can hear you. It's his first time here.'

The black man guffawed and stared at him. Even the laugh sounded musical. He improvised a guaracha with a single phrase: 'The night is young . . . the night is young.' After that a couple asked him to sing a bolero. GG went over to the musician and put a dollar in one of the tins that contained coins. At that moment someone clasped him by the arm in a friendly fashion:

'Are you enjoying yourself, Mr Greene?'

It was Robert Tripp. Impeccable. He smelt of cologne. He looked like an elegant gentleman, not a policeman. Above all, he looked out of place.

'Good evening, Mr Tripp. What a surprise. Are you following me?'

They sat at a table and ordered rum. Tripp took his time replying.

'OK, I'll tell you the truth. I have an agent following you. I don't think they mean to eliminate you, but I had a feeling that they would try to contact you.'

'Why did you get that feeling?'

'They are looking for publicity. They want to cause an international scandal by killing Nazis.'

'And you want to gag them. But you won't be able to do much with such an inefficient agent.'

'You and two men disappeared in the crowd at Coney Island. My agent is very young and inexperienced. Did anything happen?'

'No, no.'

'Ha ha ha. Not very convincing. You're a terrible actor.'

'They just wanted to talk to me. They do indeed want me to write something about them. They talked for a couple of minutes. It was very quick.'

'Did they give you any information?'

'No.'

'I get the feeling that you do not want to co-operate with us, Mr Greene.'

'Many years ago, I adopted the philosophy of not meddling, Mr Tripp. Not meddling. Here I am the uninvited guest.'

'Very convenient for you.'

'I'm sorry. I don't want to discuss ethics either. I'd rather listen to El Chori. He is more entertaining.'

'This is a disgusting place. It smells bad. And that black man is mad. Let me invite you to a luxury casino, in the Hotel Nacional. Do you like to play the tables?'

'Mainly roulette.'

'Shall we go? There's no need to be concerned. The type of people who visit that casino have a lot of money and little time to read. They won't recognise you.'

The Cadillac was waiting a block away. Once inside, they breathed in the coolness of the air-conditioning and the rose-scented deodorant. It was much pleasanter to be here than stay in that dirty, hot, airless bar. Tripp breathed deeply, and said:

'I'm going to explain something to you, and after that we won't mention the matter again tonight. I need to have a bit of fun as well.'

'Go ahead.'

'You know, Mr Greene, that all these groups who kill for supposedly patriotic, ideological reasons always end up becoming a bunch of

79

mafiosos, terrorists or contract killers. Killing is what they do. It's as easy as lighting a cigarette. Also, we want to put some order on the island. We are very near neighbours. Disorder could disrupt the economy and the peace in this country. No disorder can be allowed. For us, Mexico and Cuba are very important. And, of course, Nazis should be judged with all the guarantees of the law. If we can try them in my country, or extradite them to Europe, that would have a very significant political impact on the international community.'

'You are a great patriot, a great American.'

'That's what they pay me for.'

'At least you're a cynic. That gives you an advantage over many of your compatriots, who are usually rather naïve.'

'I'm fifty years old, Mr Greene. I'll soon have spent thirty years as a policeman. Only a cynic can keep going without collapsing.'

'We agree on that. Come on, the roulette wheel awaits us.'

8

The following day GG got up at eight-thirty in the morning with a hangover. He'd drunk a great deal in the casino, had lost one hundred and fifty dollars at roulette and Tripp had brought him back to his hotel in the Cadillac. He had a shower, shaved and tried to stop feeling frightened. The Habash group was offering him a perfect opportunity to write an exceptional book and – for now – had not asked for anything in return. But the FBI was watching him. GG knew very well that the secret services always play dirty and put in low blows without thinking twice. 'No fair play' seems to be the slogan adopted by all intelligence and counter-intelligence services throughout the world.

The telephone rang. Robert Tripp. He was waiting to have breakfast with him, and would meet him in the hotel lobby.

'Don't you remember, Mr Greene? I think that

you were a little under the weather last night.'

'Last night I was drunk. I don't like euphemisms. Did we agree to have breakfast together?'

'I told you about the American Club and said that I'd take you there today.'

'I'll be down in a minute.'

After they'd greeted each other, Tripp said:

'I've also got a little surprise for you after breakfast. A present.'

'You don't seem the generous sort.'

'In fact, we're going to share it. It's a present for both of us. We should have our breakfast quickly.'

They walked to Prado and Virtudes. The American Club was a solid stone building, with two bars, a restaurant, a billiard room, a library and well-ventilated, comfortable, elegant rooms. They had breakfast in twenty minutes, scarcely saying a word, and then went out again onto the Paseo del Prado. The Cadillac was waiting for them. They got into the back and Tripp told the driver to go to Trocadero.

They stopped at 264 Trocadero. They were in the Colón neighbourhood, the red-light area, and it was scarcely nine-thirty in the morning. Everyone was asleep, of course. There were very few people on the street at that hour. The Cadillac moved off. It always waited a certain discreet distance away. In the corner bar, two men in civilian clothes were watching developments. One of them nodded at Tripp. A barely perceptible movement. Tripp said to GG:

'Walk behind me and keep your eyes open.'

They entered the building. The only other person was a very old and almost blind black woman sitting on a small bench next to the door of her room. It would have been a splendid stately home in colonial times. It had an enormous patio in the centre and on two floors around it were small rooms where dozens of people lived crowded together. Tripp stopped in front of the third door on the left and examined it. He pushed it gently and saw that it was flimsy. He didn't think twice. He kicked it with the heel of his shoe. He half-opened the door and went in. He had a gun in his hand. The interior was very dark, warm and humid. There were no windows. It was like a cell. GG looked in carefully. A very effeminate man's voice cried out:

'Ayyy, what's happening! Rape, rape!'

It was Superman. He was lying on an old bed,

naked, clinging onto another man. They were both very scared. Superman sat up in bed, terrified. The man jumped up and went to reach for his clothes. Tripp stepped in front of him, aiming his gun:

'Sit on the bed and keep calm. Both of you, keep calm.' He spoke to GG: 'Please, come in and close the door. We need to speak to these two gentlemen.'

Keeping the gun pointed at the bed, Tripp went over to a light hanging from the ceiling. He pulled a cord and lit it. The room was dismal, the walls were damp and chipped. The bed was a jumble of dirty sheets. The guy that was with Superman was very white, thin and short. He must have been about forty. Tripp and GG recognised him immediately. It was George Greene.

Tripp took his time, as always, to adjust his eyes to the darkness, and for everyone to know who was in control of the situation. He looked for a chair. There wasn't one. Only that old bed and a few cardboard boxes in the corner, and some string stretching between two nails. There were some clothes on hangers attached to the string. That was all. George Greene kept quiet and bit his lip. Superman trembled with fear and whined:

'Ay, I've done nothing, for the love of God. Don't kill me. I've done nothing.'

'Be quiet.'

Silence returned to the tiny room. Tripp took out his FBI badge and showed it.

'You are suspects in a murder case and you are in a lot of trouble.'

George Greene said:

'We are out on bail.'

'Be quiet. I'm not interested. Let's begin with you. I want you to answer three questions clearly, without beating about the bush: Who are you really? Why did you pass yourself off as Graham Greene? And what happened on the night of July 16 in the dressing room of this gentleman in the Shanghai Theatre? Begin. And be precise. I don't have much time.'

'Could you stop pointing your gun at me?'

'No.'

'Errr . . . OK. My name is George Greene, I'm a journalist. Or rather, I was a journalist for the *Liverpool Star Weekly* until a few days ago. I came to Havana to have a bit of fun and . . . well, I thought that I might find a job here and stay a while. I need some changes in my life because . . .'

'Stop, I'm not interested in that. Why did you pass yourself off as Graham Greene?'

'It wasn't intentional. What happened was, I arrived at the hotel, I asked for a room, I gave my passport to the man on the desk and when he heard my surname, he became excited. He spoke to me in perfect English and told me he had read all my books. He didn't give me time to react. He made me sign a novel that he was reading and repeated that I was his favourite writer. He got confused.'

'And why did you go along with it?'

'I felt flattered. He even offered me a special room.'

'And a bottle of Scotch on the house.'

'How do you know that?'

'I'm the one asking the questions.'

'All right.'

'What happened in that dressing room? What went on?'

'Nothing. I went to look for Charity . . . um, Superman. I went in through the back door. There's a doorman there. A fat old bloke who talks incessantly. I remember that I gave him a dollar tip and he let me through. The dressing-room door was open. I went in. I turned on the light and waited a few minutes. Then Superman arrived and we hardly spoke because he saw a pool of blood under some boxes, in a corner. He moved the boxes, thinking it was some sort of witchcraft, and he discovered the body. We didn't do anything. I hardly saw the body. I'm afraid of the dead.'

Superman was keeping quiet, but he could not contain himself. He was trembling with fear. He moaned:

'Oh my God, but we didn't do anything. I didn't do anything, nor did he.'

Tripp put an abrupt halt to the moaning and groaning:

'Be quiet, you idiot!'

He spoke to GG: 'Is there anything you want to ask?'

'Yes. Mr George Greene, I would like you to tell me what you did on that Liverpool weekly?'

'Errr, I was a journalist.'

'What sort?'

'Errr . . . I worked in the editorial office.'

'What did you do in that office?'

'Are all these details necessary?'

'Yes. Answer me.'

'I wrote replies to readers' letters, the horoscope, cookery recipes and a section on advice for housewives.'

'And you gave up such an interesting job?'

'Don't make fun of me.'

'And what are you thinking of doing now?'

'I always wanted to be a sailor, to write travel books, adventure novels, perhaps here, in the port . . .'

'But you don't have any documentation or money.'

'I think I lost my passport. I spent all my money on the bail.'

Tripp took an envelope out of the inside pocket of his jacket and gave it to him:

'I am returning your passport. You are in the clear with the FBI. The Cuban police are your concern.'

Tripp went to the door, opened it and walked off without looking back, followed by GG. When they were out on the street, he said:

'This world is full of imbeciles.'

'We're all a bit stupid. Don't you ever try to understand other people?'

'Just understanding myself is difficult enough,

Mr Greene. It's usually impossible. Can I take you anywhere? I have time and a Cadillac at my disposal.'

'No, thank you. Thanks for the gift. And for the breakfast.'

'OK. We'll be in touch.'

'Goodbye, Mr Tripp.'

GG walked along Trocadero towards Prado. The pimps and the prostitutes were sleeping. Many bars were still closed. For a moment it seemed to him that he was in a country of madmen, to which all the other madmen in the world were heading. However, to all appearances, Cuba seemed like a normal country.

9

GG strolled round the neighbourhood for a while. There were a lot of shops, theatres, cinemas, bookshops, all kinds of businesses, and buildings under construction. The city was throbbing with activity. He remembered the beautiful old pornographic photos that the police had confiscated in George Greene's room. He headed towards Neptuno. There were at least twenty second-hand bookshops next to each other. They sold everything, at cheap prices: old books, coins, banknotes and stamps for collectors, and all kinds of pornography. He took his time and chose carefully. He finally bought two albums with postcards from the early years of the century. They were beautiful photographs of naked men and women.

He went back to the American Club. It was eleven in the morning and the heat was already intolerable. GG was a rather delicate man, not built for physical exercise. He went to the bar, ordered a gin and tonic and began reading *The Times*. He couldn't concentrate, and only read a few headlines. He was attracted by the idea of writing a book with the information that the Habash group could give him. *Nazi Hunters* might be an evocative title. But they would surely put pressure on him to sing their praises and give them heroic status. GG hated writing about heroes and heroic stances. It's a false concept. There have never been heroes throughout the history of humanity. It's an idea that was conceived to manipulate the gullible masses, a misleading concept adored by politicians and military men. And it's mainly the most egocentric and petulant people who love the idea, people who aspire to go down in history and become immortalised in statues and on the back of coins.

The members of the Habash group were acting for a variety of reasons: money, a desire for vengeance and justice, and the pleasure of killing. And who knows how many other equally petty motives each individual member might have. GG knew that they would pressure him to give a monolithic view of them: heroes in search of justice, perfect avengers, hewn from a single block of steel.

He ordered another gin and tonic. On a small table next to his chair there was a weekly programme for the racecourse. Oriental Park. He needed to relax a bit. The past few days had been intense. But several ideas were forming in his head. He often took note of them. Sometimes a university would ask him to give a lecture, and it was preferable to have written notes. He wrote in a small notebook:

The Virtue of Disloyalty

Disloyalty is a writer's privilege. Isn't it the story-teller's task to act as the devil's advocate, to elicit sympathy and understanding for those who lie outside the boundaries of State approval, because these people are badly treated or might be badly treated. My duty and the meaning of my commitment is to be a piece of grit in the State machinery. I prefer a political enemy to someone who is indifferent. Politics is part of the air that we breathe. What interests me in political figures are not their political ideas, but why they apply them. What interests me is the 'human factor'.

That was enough. When he got back to Capri he could think a bit more, round out and extend these notes and write a several-page essay. He went to the restaurant, had braised veal and boiled vegetables with two glasses of wine. He looked at the racecourse programme again. The races started at five in the afternoon. He went to the Bristol. He had an hour's siesta and woke refreshed. He felt much calmer. Writing and thinking made him feel stronger. A day in which he did not write something, whatever it might be, was for him a day wasted.

At five on the dot he went into Oriental Park. They let him through to take a look at the stables from a distance. A dollar opened a lot of doors in this city. The attendant stayed beside him and only let him be there for a few minutes. He liked the look of Dolores, a Mexican horse that was being saddled up for the second race. Sometimes he believed in his telepathic instincts. He bet fifty dollars. The horse came in fifth. For the third race he fancied Old Black, a very young horse, just in from New Orleans, with good form. He bet fifty dollars. Old Black led for the first circuit, then got tired and fell behind. It came in sixth. GG became discouraged. He went to the bar. He ordered a very cold Miller. It was an American beer. Very light. He didn't like it. The evening was not turning out as it should. A guy came up to him. He was a thin, malnourished black man, short and badly dressed. He spoke in a mixture of English and Spanish and was good humoured and self-assured.

'Hey, mister, good morning.'

'Good afternoon.'

'Oh yes, afternoon, ha ha ha. Do you want to back a winner in the next race?'

'That's what we all want. Always.'

'For two dollars I'll give you the name.'

'Oh no, that's all I need.'

'It's a certainty, mister. It's all fixed and I have good contacts. Give me two dollars and if you win, give me another ten.'

'And what if I lose?'

'You can't lose. It's a sure thing.'

'Do they always fix things like this here?'

'Here, and everywhere, mister. Everything's

fixed in this shitty world. Don't believe in luck, don't believe in honesty, don't believe in anything.'

'Hey, hey, stop.'

'Let me give you some advice: put yourself in with the winners and don't let them kick you out on your arse. The ones on top are the ones in charge.'

'They must have thrown you out of that group some time back.'

'Yes, mister. You get bad moments in life sometimes. But you should have seen me a few years ago in Madison Square Garden. Do you know who I am?'

'No.'

'I was lightweight champion of the world.'

'Oh, please.'

'Don't you believe me? Do I look rough?'

'Yes, quite rough.'

'Buy me a beer?'

'Why not?'

'Ask for Hatuey. That American beer is shit.'

'Are you a patriot?'

'No, a drunk, ha ha ha.'

When the two beers were put in front of them, they drank a toast.

'Cheers, mister.'

'Cheers, boxer.'

'Mister, don't waste time. They're going to shut the betting office. I'll also tell you who I am, so that you can trust me. I was born in Los Sitios. Do you know what Los Sitios is?'

'No.'

'One of the best neighbourhoods in Havana. A lot of very famous people come from there, musicians, boxers, baseball players. I'm El Niño Loco, Crazy Boy, they called me in Madison and in the newspapers. Haven't you heard of me?'

'Sport doesn't interest me. Especially boxing.'

'It should interest you. Boxing is life, or the other way round. Life is boxing – you hit, you get hit. And the one who wins is the one who hits the hardest and the quickest and who can take the most punishment. That's life, mister. Nothing complicated. It's all very simple. Give me two dollars and go and place your bet. You can get rich in five minutes.'

GG took out two dollars and gave them to him.

'You can place a big bet. Whatever you want. Hurry up. A good-looking Mexican horse called Centella will win.'

GG looked at the programme. Centella was in stall three, but there was no form on the horse. It just said that it was Mexican and was a three-year-old.

'Are you sure, boxer?'

'It's a certainty, mister. Run, before they close the betting windows. You're very slow. You can't go through life like that.'

'I'm cautious.'

'If you were a boxer, you'd be cowardly, chicken and slow. The trainer would throw you out of the gym on the first day. Or worse, you'd be used as a punch bag.'

'All right, OK, I'm going.'

'We're getting to be friends. Give me forty cents. I'll buy two more beers and we'll go and watch the race.'

Five minutes later GG had in his hand ten ten-dollar tickets. Centella won by a head. It was perfect. It didn't seem like a fixed race. The odds were five to one. GG was paid five hundred dollars. Crazy Boy stuck to him. GG looked at him. He didn't seem like a boxer, much less a world champion. But he had a gleam in his eye and a spring in his step. It looked as if he was waiting for the bell

97

to launch himself at his opponent. That black guy had been born to win. GG was hit by a wave of tenderness. He counted out one hundred dollars and gave them to Crazy Boy.

'Hey, mister, that's a lot . . . well, OK, hand it over. Let's have a drink. I'll invite you.'

'There are some bars across from Coney Island . . .'

'You want to go there? Let's go, mister. We're millionaires.'

'A couple of nights ago I saw some whores there . . .'

'Did you like the look of them?'

'Yes, I saw two or three that were pretty.'

'We're millionaires, mister. Let's go and look for a couple of pretty white girls. Not black. Black women bring black men bad luck. It has to be two white ones. One for you, one for me. I've been wanting some for days, but a man with no money is a piece of toilet paper.'

10

It was a splendid night. Crazy Boy went off with a good-looking, big-arsed white girl. GG took two women to his room, Clara and Mima. A mulatta and a black woman, young and flexible, who made love in front of him, smoked marijuana, got drunk and encouraged GG to take them both in every imaginable way. At three in the morning Clara went out for half an hour and brought back her husband – she didn't want to say 'my pimp' – and offered him a little show. GG had got tired and couldn't go on. They were sexual machines, unstoppable. They were having a good time and on top of that they were getting paid

GG went back to his hotel in a taxi. It was beginning to get light. He asked the taxi driver to leave him on the Malecón.

'We're a bit far away. If you don't know the city …'

'Don't worry. Thanks.'

He paid him and sat on the wall of the Malecón. He wanted to see the dawn break, have a coffee from one of those stalls and feel young and adventurous again. The sea – very calm – went from grey to blue. Now the air was fresh and transparent, and the city was silent. He'd never had such a mad and frenetic night of sex. It had been a proof. Yes. Sex is a stimulus. A black fisherman in Saint Kitts had told him this. The man was selling as aphrodisiacs the dried penises of a hawksbill, a kind of small turtle. He had bought one. He just had to scrape it with a knife. The powder was mixed with rum or coffee and taken an hour before sex. 'But the best aphrodisiac in the world is a woman you like,' the fisherman said when he left. He was right. That mulatta and that black woman got so involved and enjoyed themselves so much that they made him forget that they were whores and that they were charging for the whole thing. They were attractive and young, and also insatiable. They wanted more and more. When they saw that they couldn't count on him any longer they went to look for another man because they still wanted more.

GG had a couple of cups of coffee at a stall and decided to walk home. He asked for directions and set off. He wanted to see the city waking up, to mix with people. He felt strong and male, a conqueror. 'If I lived in Havana it would be different. Perhaps I'd think about happier things and be less anxious. This is a good place.'

He always made sure not to leave traces of his misdemeanours, especially his sexual misdemeanours. He had a deep-seated sense of Christian guilt. 'Living here would be a good therapy against the idea of sin. It's an obsolete concept, but I can't get free of it,' he thought with a smile as he went up the hill on G Street and smelt the oleander mixed with the soot from the diesel engines of the first buses of the day, which were already crowded.

After having a shower and putting on clean clothes, he felt hungry. He went to the American Club for breakfast. It was nine in the morning. He wanted to look through the papers and think about going back. Two or three days' rest here would do him good. Perhaps he could visit the beaches to the east of the city. And, of course, repeat the party with Clara and Mima. He was beginning to like the city. A bit excessive and chaotic, but lack of balance is stimulating. The totally predictable equilibrium of his life in Capri bored and depressed him.

He thought about all this while he was having his breakfast. He was interrupted by a tall, slim, attractive woman, around forty. She spoke perfect English.

'Oh, Mr Greene?'

'Yes.'

'Forgive me for interrupting your thoughts.'

'You're interrupting my breakfast.'

'And your thoughts, which are more important. Your mind is very far from this table. Let me introduce myself: my name's Loretta King, from New York. I'm a professor at the Commercial University in Havana.'

'A pleasure to meet you. Would you like a cup of tea? Sit down, please.'

'I'd rather have a coffee.'

They ordered coffee for Loretta.

'As you might imagine, Mr Greene, I always read your books. I think I have all of them. You are my favourite writer . . . favourite living writer, that is.'

'Thank you. And which dead writers do you like?'

'That's a long list. I think it changes according to my mood, but I would be delighted to invite you to lunch at my house. We could talk more peacefully there. This place ...'

'The American Club is perfect. It seems like a piece of Boston transplanted to the Caribbean.'

'My house is much better. Do you like lobster with celery, in an oyster sauce? Or would you prefer prawns in pineapple juice on a bed of apples? They are my two specialities. It would be a pleasure to cook for you.'

'You are too kind.'

'Here's my card. What about midday today?'

'Very well, I accept.'

'Then I will leave you to continue with your breakfast and your thoughts. I'll see you later.'

GG made light of it. He was used to meetings of this sort. He usually did not accept invitations from admirers, and had a long list of polite refusal lines. But it was sometimes pleasant to allow himself to be trapped or, at least, to chat for a while. Find out about other lives. All in all, this was his job: to find out how other people lived, what happened to them, mix it all up, add a few drops of his own and write novels. A strange job. A novelist is like a priest. They both base the success of their work on people's credulity. They have to make an effort to be convincing. People visiting them have to believe it all. Absolutely everything. Without a chink of doubt. However impossible the story they are told.

He spent the rest of the morning strolling around. He bought deodorant, eau de cologne and scented soap, to fit in with tropical customs. In the tropics people are obsessed with hygiene and perfume to fight the smell of sweat and putrefaction.

At twelve precisely, he arrived at Loretta's home: a penthouse in the Royal Palm building on the Malecón. The lift was impeccable, with bronzes and mirrors. He walked up a few impressive white marble stairs, and everything shone and seemed recently finished. Loretta was waiting for him. She now looked even more attractive. She had records of the latest American music: Frank Sinatra, Paul Anka, Gershwin, Stanley Black. They drank Martinis and looked out at the sea. Loretta had a spacious terrace high above the street. It had a perfect view of the city, the Caribbean and the port entrance. They talked about simple things: her work at the university, her preferred authors and GG's books. He avoided talking about himself. Perhaps it was just shyness, but he felt uncomfortable when his books were praised in his presence. She realised this and after two Martinis, she asked:

'Do you like photography, Mr Greene?'

'Not particularly.'

'It's my hobby. Would you like to see some of my work?'

'Fine.'

She showed him an album with more than two hundred black and white photos. Not very artistic. They were all of black men, completely naked. Most of them had erect penises. GG was not expecting this and gave a start. Loretta laughed coquettishly:

'In Havana you can commit every imaginable sin. I like committing them. One after the other. Incessantly.'

'I can see that.'

'It looks as if you are not having a very good time. You should relax and enjoy Havana. Then you'll fall in love with the city and you'll have to come back often. This city is feminine, my dear Graham. May I call you Graham?'

'Yes.'

'This city is a big whore. It's seductive, hypnotic, and it envelops you. And if you don't put up any resistance, you'll stay for ever.'

'Is this what happened to you?'

'Mine's a long and complicated story. Better leave it for another occasion. Besides, Graham, I don't have time. I hate rushing things, but ...'

GG stiffened and looked at her in surprise.

'Oohh, ha ha ha – it isn't what you think! Don't get me wrong, but ever since I tried black men, I can't stand white men in my bed. At least, the white men in my country are completely predictable and . . .'

'You don't seem very Anglo-Saxon.'

'I've lived here for years. Perhaps the Cubans have contaminated me. And then I'm from the south. I was born in Tampa. My family still lives there. I think that I'm Anglo-Saxon and therefore very pragmatic, Graham. Absolutely pragmatic.'

'So am I. Romantic people are at a disadvantage.'

'I agree. Would you like another Martini? A whisky?'

'No thanks, I'm fine.'

'Before we eat, I want to tell you something. I'll be brief.'

'Go ahead.'

'I work for the Communist International.'

'Ahhh.'

'Does that surprise you? Obviously. As you can imagine, I'm telling you a secret that could cost me my life. I'm a professional.'

GG was prepared for anything except that. He kept quiet.

'You were a member of the British Communist Party.'

'For just four weeks. In 1923. A long time ago.'

'Exactly thirty-two years ago. We know that you are what is called a "critical sympathiser". An ambiguous term. In any event, you are the card we have in hand and we want to play that card.'

'I'm nobody's playing card.'

'The KGB has an excellent dossier with some details of your life. Did you know that?'

'So have MI6 and the FBI. It doesn't bother me at all.'

'I only told you for general information. Don't get annoyed. We'll leave that to one side. We'd like your help, with no strings. We could offer you certain advantages . . .'

'Get to the point, please.'

'The KGB could provide you with enough secret material for you to write a book that could be dynamite at this moment in the Cold War.'

'What do you want from me?'

'We know that the Habash group has contacted you. We need you to infiltrate them and work for us.'

'A double agent?'

'Exactly.'

'That's the most dangerous job in your profession, Miss Kent. Why are you asking me to do it?'

'It is not in our interests to have them going on killing Nazis on the run who are living in the Americas.'

'Why?'

'You ask too many questions, my dear Graham, but I can answer you: we have them under control. When we decide, we can take them over to the USSR and try them as war criminals. That would have a major political effect.'

GG did not speak but he thought: 'That's what the United States is thinking of doing. God creates them and the devil brings them together.'

'Let me explain something else: we have tried to talk to the Habash group, but they don't want to.

They are unhinged. Unfortunately we do not have the resources here to eliminate them – I mean, neutralise them. We don't even know how many there are or where they have their main base. We need someone we can trust inside the group. Do you understand now why I said that you are the only card that we have in our hand?'

'I understand.'

'I repeat that your payment would be most enticing. I'm going to break the rules and give you an advance. I'm confident that I'm talking to a man who knows how to keep quiet when necessary. When you make the first move, I will give you a thick dossier with photocopies of Operation Paper Clip. You'll write a thrilling book, an international best-seller. All the documents are unpublished and classified Top Secret by both sides since 1945.'

'Could you say a bit more?'

'In May 1945, American troops occupied Peenemünde and other installations where the Nazis researched, built and launched their bombs, the famous V-2s that were used to bomb London. Those were the babies. There was a lot more. The director of the entire Hitler rocket programme was Wernher von Braun. Well, the US government dismantled it all and took everything up to the last screw, including, of course, all the scientists and specialist workers. It was a perfect and very secret operation. They spend millions of dollars every month to control space and they think that they can land on the Moon soon. If they install a rocket launcher on the moon . . . Anyway, the USSR is very anxious that a writer like you should tell this story to the world in a book. They use these Nazi scientists with a complete disregard for ethics and..'

'Please, Miss Kent, this was the spoils of war. This is what warmongers have always done: they carry off what they can, and burn and destroy the rest. We are civilised beings.'

'Ohh . . .'

'The USSR would have done the same if they had got to Peenemünde first.'

'OK, I agree. Ethics is not our speciality, Graham. At least, not mine. But I repeat: if you agree to work with us, you will receive all the dossiers on this operation.'

GG knew, suddenly, that he was caught in the crossfire of three groups: the FBI, Habash and the

KGB. He decided to play for time.

'Ummm, I'd need to think about it.'

'I urge you to make a quick decision. I'll show you a copy of a confidential document that the President of the Republic received some days ago:

> Central Intelligence Agency
> Washington DC
> Office of the Director
> 15 July 1955

His Excellency General Fulgencio
Batista Zaldívar
President of the Republic of Cuba
Havana, Cuba

Dear Mr President

I remember with great pleasure our meeting held during my trip to Havana last April. For me it was a great honor to have had the pleasurable and interesting experience of visiting you.

The creation by the Cuban government of the Bureau for Repression of Communist Activities is a great step forward in the cause of Liberty. I feel honored that your government has agreed to permit this Agency to assist in the training of some of the officers of this important organization.

As you will remember from our conversations last April, I established that this Agency would feel honored to assist in the training of the personnel that you would send as you wish. I understand that General Martín Díaz Tamayo will direct the activities of the Bureau for Repression of Communist Activities and he will be responsible for its organization. In this case I would like to suggest that it might be advisable for General Díaz Tamayo to come to Washington in the near future, so that we might be able to discuss the activities of international communism. I am sure that it would be useful to exchange opinions with General Díaz Tamayo as a prelude to the group of his subordinates who will come here to train. The material we will offer could be of considerable help in his task of organizing the Bureau for Repression of Communist Activities. We will indicate to him as well the type of officer that he should prefer when selecting individuals for training.

In view of the interest that the Minister of State, Dr Carlos Saladrigas, expressed about this matter, I am taking the liberty of writing him today, pointing out to him the ideas contained in this letter. I will suggest to him, if it is acceptable to you and your government, that he extend an invitation in my name to General Díaz Tamayo so that he may come to Washington for approximately two weeks, preferably beginning the first of August. I trust that this will meet with your approval.

Allow me to say again, Mr President, what a great honor and pleasure it has been to meet and talk with you, and I trust that we will be in a position to assist you and your country in our mutual efforts against the enemies of Liberty.

Please accept, once again, Mr President, my very best wishes.

Sincerely

Allen Dulles, Director.

'You are very effective, Miss Kent.'
'Not me. The cause. We have friends everywhere.'

'So I see.'

'It's clear that they are going to take strong repressive measures against the Communists. By my reckoning we have one or two months to act. No more. The United States is moving quickly to consolidate its position here.'

'But the Cubans wouldn't allow ...'

'Cubans allow anything if there's money involved. The dollar is in charge here. But tomorrow the rouble could be in charge. It would make no difference whoever the president might be. So, in short, we are preparing to leave this city and strike a hard blow as a parting gift. We want to liquidate Habash and take a big group of Nazis over to the USSR for trial in Moscow.'

'And would you leave this place peacefully?'

'Things come and go. It's best not to know so much. It's unhealthy in this business.'

'I know.'

'In any case, let me tell you something: this is a conflict area with the United States. As important as Mexico. Now we have to make a tactical withdrawal, but we'll take it over again, in a much more solid way, with a long-term strategy. It's just a question of money and finding a strong and clever politician who knows how to get things done. This is a poor country with no natural resources. It will always need money to subsist, whatever the source.'

'I don't think it's just a question of money. Communist ideology . . ?'

'Ideology and politics are just the anaesthetic in the operation. The scalpel is money. Don't be naïve, Graham. What makes the world go around is money and politicians' desire for power. It's always been like that, ever since the first leader emerged in a cave. Good intentions don't work. It's the dark side of human beings – ambition, vanity, egocentricity, the desire for wealth and power – that makes the planet work. Good people don't move anything along, they retreat up a mountain to pray to gods that they invent.'

'You've learned a lot in the KGB.'

'We are much more objective in the KGB than the US Communist Party is. And we call things by their name, openly, not beating around the bush. Politicians have to repeat so many lies every day that they end up believing them and deceiving themselves.'

'Very well, miss, thank you for your lessons. I

think I'll never forget them. But I'm hungry.'

'We'll eat straight away. When will you be able to give me an answer?'

'In two or three days. I'll come and see you.'

They ate lobsters and celery in an oyster sauce sitting on the terrace, overlooking the green and blue Caribbean. The heat and the sun were suffocating. Black clouds were appearing from the south and east, bringing the promise of refreshing showers for the evening.

11

The lunch, the alcohol and the intolerable heat at three in the afternoon were a perfect soporific. GG thought that a walk along the Malecón would do him good. Dozens of ragged children were splashing in the pools. Some dared to swim out to sea, although word had it that sharks came close to the shore because the water was deep. It was incredible what was happening. It seemed like a dream. Or a nightmare. In this short space of time he had received two very attractive proposals to write a couple of books. Each of them dangerous. And he had the FBI on his heels. Perhaps MI6 was also watching him.

'No, Graham, keep calm. You have to avoid these persecution manias. You need to sleep a bit so that you can see everything more clearly,' he thought. At that moment a car drew up beside him. A Chevrolet, the latest model. The man who had contacted him in the café and then met him at the gates of Coney Island got out. Now he gave him no time to do anything. He came up to him quickly, and put his arms around his shoulders, smiling. He seemed to be greeting an old friend that he had met by chance. Very effusive and friendly. Nobody would think that he was a common murderer. Still smiling, he gently pushed him towards the car. He muttered:

'Good afternoon, Mr Greene. How are you? Come with us. Come on. Don't resist. We want to take you for a drive round the city. Let's go, and keep quiet. Smile and get into the car.'

GG felt afraid and could scarcely stop himself trembling. He decided not to speak so that they wouldn't realise that his voice was also trembling. The car moved off slowly, taking its time. There was just the driver, the smiling man and him. Everyone silent. Finally GG spoke out:

'I want you to explain to me . . .'

'There's nothing to explain. Don't be scared, nothing's going to happen to you.'

The man was now using a persuasive tone. He seemed calm and serene. They drove for half an hour through streets choked with traffic. GG did not know it, but they were heading towards El Cotorro, in the south-east of the city. They drove into a dingy alley and changed cars, with the same occupants. They picked out a complicated route through the neighbourhood streets before joining the main road again and heading back towards La Virgen del Camino. The guy sitting next to him told him to get down on the floor, and blindfolded him.

'Don't worry. Nothing's going to happen to you. Keep calm.'

GG was sweating profusely. It was very hot. The car windows were wound up and he was getting more and more nervous. He had an attack of claustrophobia and almost cried out, but he contained himself, clenching his teeth and praying. He gradually calmed down and kept praying incessantly. He felt the car make several turns and head down a stony, unpaved road full of potholes.

It finally stopped. He heard voices. They took off his blindfold and told him to get out. The Captain was standing solidly in front of him, his legs apart, his arms crossed, staring quizzically. He was wearing a baseball cap and dark glasses and was smoking a cigar. He loved playing the supermacho. He smiled at him sardonically and held out his hand.

'Welcome, Mr Greene. Forgive me the inconvenience I am causing you. Would you like a soft drink?'

'No.'

'Yes, why not? Please have one because you might get dehydrated. You are sweating a lot. Were the boys rough? I hope not. I told them that they should invite you to meet me pleasantly, ha ha ha.'

GG looked around him. He was standing in a spacious and cool farm set in the middle of an extensive grove of mango, avocado, mamey, guayaba and orange trees. A pretty place, quiet and isolated, on the outskirts of the city. There was just the sound of birdsong. He tried to take a good look and pick out some points of reference. He had now got himself under control again. The Captain said:

'Don't worry. This is a quiet place and you are in good hands. Come with me.'

Once inside, they headed to the dining room of the house. The Captain opened a couple of bottles of fizzy drink. One for each of them. He gave him the bottle without a glass. They drank quickly.

'Would you like another? Or would you prefer mineral water?'

'Water.'

He took a bottle of mineral water out of the fridge, opened it and handed it to him. They remained standing.

'I'm sorry. I don't have any alcohol here.'

'No need.'

'Come along. There's air-conditioning in this room.'

They went across to another room. The house was furnished and it looked as if a family lived there. The Captain opened the door with two keys. The solid door had two locks. The room was large and cool and it had a big table and six chairs. In one corner were three metal filing cabinets, each with four large drawers. Alongside them were some wooden boxes, containing weapons. The Captain said:

'Come over here. You're a privileged man. I want to show you all this.'

He opened several boxes. They were full of machine guns, handguns, grenades and rockets, all new and in mint condition.

'This is our arsenal. Or rather, part of our arsenal.

We have others like this in different parts of the country and in other countries. We have everything, all first-class quality. All that's missing is a tank battalion.'

GG kept silent. The man was trying to impress him.

'Now come and look at this.'

He opened some drawers in the filing cabinets. They were crammed with files, organised alphabetically. Each one had its own name in German.

'Please, take any file. Whichever you want.'

GG did so. There were photos, copies of identity papers, addresses, telephone numbers, a history of the person, a psychological profile, his weak points, his interests and vices, family letters. Everything.

GG had worked in MI6 during the Second World War, until 1944. He knew that compiling that enormous amount of information, in secret, was the work of professionals with plenty of resources. Not a bunch of amateurs or layabouts, or a group of common killers. The Captain was expecting praise.

'What do you think?'

'Very professional. I congratulate you.'

'Is that all?'

'What do you want? You want me to nominate you for the Nobel Peace Prize?'

'It's perfect, Mr Greene. Years of work. There are five hundred dossiers here, rigorously prepared. Five hundred war criminals. Five hundred and eleven to be precise, people living in this continent. And this archive is growing bit by bit. Every day there is some new item. We are very efficient. I calculate, and this is my own personal calculation, that there are several thousand of them living peacefully in Latin America. And they have no right to live. They only have a right to die.'

'From what I can see, you are as precise as the Nazis.'

'We are rigorous. Don't compare us with those animals.'

The Captain got up from his chair and walked around quietly. He wanted to give GG time to think. After a long silence, GG finally made up his mind.

'This archive is very tempting.'

'That's why we brought you here. Seeing is believing. It's a simple proposition: every time Habash eliminates a Nazi, you will immediately receive a copy of the personal dossier of that criminal. And about the group, you'll only be able to write what I tell you. Not a word more.'

'That's a simple rule.'

'It's very simple, but if you break it, you will pay with your life, wherever you might be hiding. You already know that Habash does not believe in forgiveness.'

'You're very direct.'

'I'm a pragmatic man.'

'From what I can see, we're all pragmatic. There are no romantics left in the world.'

'What's your answer?'

'I have to think. I need some time . . .'

'Is that a no?'

'No. I'm just asking for time.'

'Take all the time you need, but if you decide not to collaborate with our cause, the only thing you must do is to forget completely and for ever what you have seen and heard in our company. I am a military man. Do you understand what I'm saying?'

'Err . . . well.'

'What I mean is I'm inflexible, and I don't show pity or compassion.'

'Very well.'

'I'm going to leave you alone in this room for fifteen minutes. I'll wait for you outside. Look through the archive if you like. Whatever you want. That will help you to decide. I think that I'm being very generous here, Mr Greene. I don't recognise myself.'

The Captain left the room abruptly, without waiting for a reply. GG went over to the filing cabinets and looked through a few dossiers. Out of the corner of his eye, he glanced at the big mirror in the gold frame on the opposite wall. They'd be watching him through that mirror. All the dossiers had too much information – it was unnecessary to do all that work just to put a bullet in these people's heads. They were obsessive, and therefore dangerous. GG went over to a large window with a grille that overlooked the orchard. The Captain was strolling among the trees, meditating. He was looking at the ground and walking slowly and silently on his own. GG thought that he seemed a character condemned to a tragic fate. He was brave, charismatic, intelligent, astute, obsessive, ambitious and energetic. He had all the qualities of a tragic figure. He would have liked to write a novel based on this person, a man who was implacable and dangerous at this moment in time. A ferocious jackal who would slowly lose his strength and become disillusioned and disappointed. His superiors – there are always superiors, whoever they might be – were now using him as the military head of their revenge operations. After that they would discard him, and he would end up fleeing terrified from country to country. With a lot of money, but alone and mad, pursued by the ghosts of those he had killed, and trailed by the people who had used him. His torment would finally end with a bullet to the head. He was just the gun. Not the hand that controlled the gun.

The door opened. One of the Captain's men asked him:

'Are you ready to go back?'

'Yes.'

They went out onto the patio. The Captain came up to say goodbye.

'I'm not giving up hope that we'll have you here as our guest. Working. This is a very pleasant place.'

'Good . . . Let's see.'

'Would you like to join us on our next operation?

We are going to execute a very prominent Nazi. He's living here selling soda water. It will be amusing because we know that he will piss himself and shit in his pants before dying, literally – ha ha ha! I can just imagine the disgust of the people from the morgue when they come and pick up the body.'

'You seem very sadistic.'

'And you seem too intellectual. Which is worse?'

GG kept a cautious silence. There was rage in the Captain's eyes. He was completely intolerant, but he controlled himself. He smiled and held out his hand to GG:

'It will be a pleasure to welcome you whenever you like. I am at your disposal.'

GG shook his hand and got into the car. It was the same team that had brought him half an hour earlier. They blindfolded him and went through the same drill in reverse. When they took off the blindfold and ordered him to sit quietly on the seat, they said:

'We'll leave you here. Take a taxi and go back to your hotel.'

They left him at the Central Railway Station. GG took a taxi and headed to the Bristol. There were loud, grotesque rumbles of thunder. Suddenly there was a biblical downpour, with a lot of wind and much thunder and lightning. In a few minutes it turned cooler. He realised then that he'd been suffering the whole day as if he'd been in a sauna. This was a deluge. The streets flooded in minutes. He had a headache and felt more confused than ever before in his life. He left word in reception that he should not be disturbed for any reason. He went to bed and fell asleep immediately.

12

He woke up and looked at his watch. Ten-thirty at night. He had slept six hours and felt much clearer. What should he do? He didn't think twice. He picked up the phone and asked to be put through to the airport.

'Is there a plane leaving soon for Miami, New York or Chicago?'

'The mail plane is leaving at six in the morning for New York and it stops in Miami. It only takes twenty passengers.'

'Is there anything before that?'

'No, sir.'

'Can I reserve a seat? To New York?'

'Your name?'

'Graham Greene.'

'You've got to be at the desk half an hour early to pay for your reservation. Otherwise you'll lose the booking.'

'That's fine. Thank you.'

He rang off and did some calculations. He had seven hours in front of him. 'This is the only solution. Get away from this madness as soon as possible because it could get even more complicated,' he thought.

He had a shower and shaved. He gathered up his few belongings and put them in his bag. At the bottom of the bag he found the Somerset Maugham book. He put it on the chest of drawers and thought: 'I'm not going to carry this ridiculous rubbish half-way round the world.' He picked it up again and threw it into the waste bin. He checked out of the hotel, paid and took a taxi. It would do him good to spend a few hours in the bars on the beach, have a sandwich, drink and take in the atmosphere. He didn't feel like having sex that night. At least, not in any active way. He had been an almost professional voyeur since adolescence. But that night he didn't want even that. He felt exhausted inside. 'I've reached the age when sex isn't the problem so much as old age and death. I wake up with these in mind and not a woman's body,' he had written in *The Quiet American*. He remembered it perfectly because Fowler in that novel had too many of his characteristics.

He got out of the taxi carrying his small bag. He looked for the dive where El Chori performed and went in. He sat at a table in a dark corner. As usual, it was hot and smelt of smoke, urine and dirt. He ordered a rum. When the waiter went off, he called him back:

'What's the best rum you have?'

'Matusalen añejo'

'Bring me a bottle. And plenty of ice.'

He felt like drinking a lot. At that moment Crazy Boy came in, dressed in a white drill suit, happy, laughing, accompanied by two beautiful white women with big buttocks and breasts. He was fondling them both at the same time and they were smiling. He gave El Chori a bill to keep him playing and looked round for an empty table. GG held up his hand to attract his attention. Crazy Boy came over, still holding the two women by the waist. He was a happy man. He laughed out loud:

'Hey, mister, I'm a millionaire again! Ha ha ha!'

'How?'

'With that money you gave me. I had twenty dollars left today, and I backed a winner, ha ha ha. It paid ten to one. And here I am, dancing and having a good time. Shall we do it again tomorrow?'

'I don't think so.'

'There are some good races tomorrow, mister. And I bring you luck. I'm the Black Angel of Oriental Park!'

'Sit down and have a drink. I'm buying.'

The three of them sat down, asked for glasses and poured themselves a drink.

'What's the matter, mister? Are you worried about something?'

'I think I'm leaving early in the morning.'

'But you don't want to go.'

'I don't want to, but I have to. The sooner the better.'

'But if you want to stay, then stay. We can make a lot of money together, mister. It's a great deal. You have to be one of the winners.'

'You never know who the winners and the losers are. The thing isn't that simple.'

'Life is a boxing match, if ...'

'Yes, yes, I know your philosophy, but it isn't like that. Life isn't a boxing match. It's more complicated.'

'Yes, it is. And don't run away, because if you turn your back, you'll lose.'

'I don't believe you, Boy.'

'I don't know what it's like in your country, but Cuba's a country for brave people. You've always got to step up. Punching with both fists, ducking and weaving, hitting fast, not leaving an opening for the son of a bitch you're fighting. That's how it is. And that's how it'll be all your life.'

El Chori came over for a drink and heard what Crazy Boy was saying.

'Life is a rumba, Boy. A guaracha. And you have to take it as it comes. Not expect much. It's better to dance, drink and laugh. Take a lesson from me.'

'Take a lesson from you? You're a loser, Chori. You've got nothing to teach nobody. Marlon Brando, Tyrone Power, Nat King Cole, all the greats have come to this shit-hole to listen to you and they've invited you to the States, but you're still stuck here, in the shit.'

'Ahhh.'

'Why didn't you go? By now you could have had your own business, a bar in New York: El Chori's Guaracha with the Mulatas del Fuego, dancing rumba every night. And you'd be a millionaire.'

'Do you know why I didn't go?'

'No balls.'

'I'm afraid of planes.'

'You're afraid of life. You're a baby, a big coward and a fool. You don't have the big picture, like me. Me, I'm a beast. I've often gone to fight there, and I'm not afraid of nothing in life.'

'You're a bigger fool than me, Boy. You've been world champion twice. You don't even know how much money you made and you chucked it all away and ...'

'Hey, hey, stop. I didn't chuck it away. I spent it with the most beautiful women in the world, and on the rumba of life. I'm not like you, stuck playing to nobody and drinking rum when someone invites you.'

'And what about you – you've even pawned your world championship belts.'

GG interrupted to change the conversation, which seemed interminable.

'All right, OK, you are both winners and losers, fifty-fifty.'

'You're right, mister,' said El Chori. 'Nobody knows anything in this life. You live with what you're given. And that's it. Smiles and tears. Everything has its time.'

'Sing something and cut out the philosophy,

Chori. Don't try and be intelligent,' Crazy Boy exclaimed.

'What do you want to hear? What about a rumba, to cheer things up?'

They kept on drinking. An hour later Crazy Boy took his women off to a room he'd rented upstairs. He invited GG:

'Come with us, mister. I'll let you have both of them and I'll pay. I'll ask for a room with two beds.'

'No, Boy, thanks.'

'Don't say that, mister. Don't you want to do it with me? Do you like it in private? Or don't you like white women? A foursome's a lot of fun. Come on.'

'Thanks, Boy.'

'OK, rent another room and take the one you prefer.'

'No. I'm going to walk for a bit to get some air.'

'Be careful, this is a dangerous neighbourhood and you don't know your way around.'

GG went outside and bumped into Mima and Clara, looking very pretty with their tight-fitting dresses and high heels. They were almost running.

'Ay, Papi, leaving already? We rushed over

because we heard you were here.'

'Ehhh. Who told you?'

'The girls. You're a very distinguished man. All the girls remember you. Buy us a drink and let's talk a bit.'

GG looked at his watch. Half past twelve. Five hours left. Why not? Just looking at them got him in the mood. 'I think I was too bored and pessimistic when I wrote *The Quiet American,*' he thought, smiling. They had a few drinks. He rented a room and they went up.

It was much better this time because they knew each other. The two girls complimented him:

'What we like about you is that you take a long time to come. You fuck and fuck, but you keep it in. Young guys come straight away and it's all over. You're quite a gentleman.'

Total depravity. Cathy was like a blushing schoolgirl compared to these women, and Cathy was the most deviant person he'd been with up till then. They told each other their infidelities in a lot of detail when they made love, and that aroused them all the more. She liked to seduce young men, sailors, priests. And she told him everything. Mima and Clara were a lot madder and more depraved.

GG, cautiously, drank little. The two women were completely drunk and stoned, with rum and marijuana, at four in the morning. He got up, dressed and said goodbye to them. He gave them each a fifty-dollar bill. They squealed with joy. He picked up his small bag and went out onto the street looking for a taxi. Half an hour later he got out at the entrance to the airport at Rancho Boyeros. He had plenty of time to pay for his ticket, have breakfast and read the morning papers.

13

Two thick-set men in dark suits and hats were waiting for him. They came up to him looking very serious. One asked:

'Mr Graham Greene?'

'Yes.'

'Come with us.'

He tried to resist and shout out, but one of the men smiled and hugged him, as if greeting him. And at the same time he closed his enormous hand over his mouth and whispered:

'Don't make me hit you, because I'll cut your balls off right now. Shut up and walk!'

He put his arm on his shoulder. The two men smiled as if they were friends. GG looked terrified and they told him:

'Smile, you fuck, smile.'

In any event, there was nobody in the vicinity. It was four-fifty in the morning. They went towards the parking lot, got into a car and drove off. GG thought: where have these vicious guys come from? He decided not to open his mouth. He saw that they were brainless thugs. For the five years he had lived in Saigon, he had very often wished to be killed by a bullet. Phuong had been his salvation in the midst of his emotional collapse. But now he did not want to die. If everything weren't so complicated, he would like to spend a few months here. Without writing. He would just go to the racecourse and the beach bars, with those whores. He'd like to make friends with El Chori and Crazy Boy, find out how they lived. They would make very joyful characters in any novel. Havana had given him an adrenalin injection and he felt optimistic.

He started looking out of the window in a relaxed manner. 'Let it be God's will.' The car crossed the city and reached Cojímar, a small fishing village. It was still completely dark when they came up to a jetty and got onto a yacht. In the stern were two large rods for catching swordfish and sharks. An enormous, fat, but very strong man, well over six foot six tall, held out his hand with a smile:

'Welcome on board the *Black Sky*, Mr Greene. You'll have to forgive these goons, they're a bit violent, ha ha ha. I hope you'll enjoy this fishing trip. We're gonna enjoy ourselves, ha ha ha.'

He spoke English with a Bronx accent perhaps. A lot of slang. He gave order to cast off the moorings and set sail. The yacht had two powerful motors. They showed him to a small but very luxurious cabin. One of the guys said:

'If you want something to drink, there's a fridge and glasses.'

GG was hungry and thirsty. But he didn't want to eat. He had a fizzy drink and looked through the porthole as the coastline rapidly disappeared and they headed into the dark sea. He thought that the sky was getting a bit lighter.

They sailed for half an hour, at full throttle, heading north. It was dawn when the fat man opened the cabin door and called him.

'Come up on deck, Mr Greene. I want you to see something.'

GG went up. The two thugs brought a fat, pot-bellied man out of the other cabin. The man was tied up and gagged. He was about sixty and his eyes were popping out of their sockets. The skipper of the yacht concentrated on his work as if nothing was happening. The big fat man shouted an order:

'Heave to!'

The yacht stopped. The engines dawdled. The sea seemed like a silver-grey mirror. There was a very fresh, light breeze that did not ripple the surface. GG looked eastwards. It was a beautiful sunrise, with pink, orange and grey hues, and the sea slowly changed from grey to silver to blue. The fat man took out a hunting knife. He took the guy over to the side, cut him free and, at the same instant, cut his belly and threw him into the water. While the man was falling, he shouted:

'Defend yourself, you spick. I wanna see you defend yourself, ha ha ha.'

The water was stained with the man's blood. It was pumping out of the cut in his belly. He kicked and waved but could not cry out because of the gag. It was all over in a few seconds. An enormous black shark appeared. It came up quickly. It had smelt the blood. They can smell blood at enormous distances. It swerved in, head up, opened its jaws and bit off an arm and part of the shoulder of the body kicking in the water. Another shark appeared on the surface and also attacked. Horrified, GG looked away. The fat man grabbed him by the shoulders with his enormous hands and forced him to watch.

'I brought you out to see this, baby. You gotta see it all. Don't mess up my deck if you're going to puke.'

The man was already a corpse, and three sharks were tearing him apart. They were biting and thrashing to get a piece. They swallowed him all up and came back for more. GG did not know that such large and black sharks existed; they worked with terrible ferocity. There was a smell of human shit, and that was all that remained in the water along with some intestines and a few other bits, in the midst of a light-red stain that was dissolving. One of the sharks returned and swallowed the intestines with one bite. Then GG saw that he was still clutching his bag with the bits of dirty clothing. He felt small and ridiculous. He opened the bag, took out the manuscript of *The Quiet American*, put it under his arm and threw the bag into the water. It floated for just a few seconds. A shark came up like a torpedo, swerved, opened its jaws and swallowed it whole. GG smiled with satisfaction, as if he'd thrown a bone to a dog.

It no longer smelled of human excrement; the sharks disappeared into the deep. The water, now very still, caught a shaft of light as the sun appeared over the horizon; incredibly, GG felt like smiling. He smiled openly and looked at the big fat man, who also smiled and asked him:

'What? Did you like the show?'

'Hmmm.'

'You're a delicate guy. I'll introduce myself, because it's time we got to know each other before you keep on running around Havana without knowing what you're doing or where you're going, keeping bad company and putting yourself into cheap dives. My name is . . . well, it's an Italian name. It won't mean anything to you. Everyone calls me the Magician because I like to make things disappear. People usually. People that annoy me and don't wanna listen to me, I disappear them. Not even a little bone left, ha ha ha. Come with me. You want coffee?'

They went onto the top deck, sat by a small table and one of the thugs brought a tray with coffee, hot milk, bread rolls, butter and jams.

'Eat up, writer. Have some breakfast and tell me

143

what you've been up to in Havana?'

The Magician spoke with his mouth full. He swallowed everything down in two minutes. GG served himself coffee with a dash of milk, and drank it in silence.

'Don't you wanna talk, writer? Are you scared? OK, well then I'll tell you what you're thinking could happen. I could throw you to the sharks. You could get the same as that fucking spick.'

'I was going on the six o'clock plane. I'm not interested in ...'

'Don't interrupt me! I'm doing the talking! And don't try to explain anything. I know everything. Do you know why I made that spick disappear? He owned five big casinos and he controlled the numbers in a few Havana neighbourhoods. I'll explain, so you've got everything clear: the numbers is a secret lottery. Well, that spick didn't wanna do business with me. I wanna buy him out. I'm the one who controls all the casinos in Havana. All of them. And we're going to keep on. Every last billiard hall will be in the family. The thing's getting bigger, my dear little writer, it's getting bigger.'

The Magician turned towards the coast, which was appearing in the distance.

'Look, you shitty little writer. Do you see that coastline? In three or four years we're going to fill it with luxury hotels and casinos and beaches. From Havana to Varadero. A hundred miles. And quickly. We're in a hurry. Las Vegas will be left behind. The wealthy people, the true millionaires, will come here to lose their money. Las Vegas will be for the poor fuckers who bet five dollars and complain because they lose. Miami will just be a transit airport, en route to Havana. Everything big scale. Very big! Do you see now how the world works, writer? We are making a very good job of it. Do I make myself clear?'

'Yes, perfectly clear.'

'So I don't want anybody to cross me. Shark lunch. Anybody crossing me ends up here. Am I right or am I right? You have to get rid of obstacles!'

'Why are you telling me all this?'

'Because I want you to understand how it works. Havana is controlled by a mechanism. A hidden mechanism. Nobody sees it. We are the people that control Havana! So I'm giving you warning: don't cross me because I'll chew you up.'

'What do you mean? What have I got to do with anything?'

145

'Do I have to spell it out?'

'Yes.'

'Ha ha ha. A very British sense of humour. OK, I'll be brief: a group of Communists here spoke to you and another group of Nazi-hunters also spoke to you. They both want you to write something about Cuba. Denigrating, offending the Cubans, and fucking things up.'

'Not exactly. It's not about that.'

'Don't interrupt me, ever. When I speak everybody listens to me. I'm personally going to wipe out those two little groups. I'm tracking them and I'll bring them all here together and give the sharks a feast. And you're not going to write a fucking word. Not a fucking word. Cuba is a paradise, an eternal summer, sir. We're going to receive millionaire tourists. Every year millions and millions will come and leave their money here. And, of course, nothing unpleasant happens here. Here everything is perfect, Mr Greene. The people are happy and friendly, the women are beautiful, families are happy, the poor live well, the politicians love democracy and freedom, we don't have thieves or pickpockets, people don't commit suicide, everyone is educated and healthy.

Cubans always smile at life because this is a paradise. Do you understand me now?'

'Yes.'

'In a few days we're going to run our first advertising campaign. A big campaign. We've spent three million dollars. Just for the United States: "Paradise awaits you in Cuba".'

'Ahha.'

'What did you say?'

'Nothing.'

'What do you mean, nothing?'

'Nothing. I've got nothing to say. You're doing the talking.'

'I want a concrete answer from you. Right now! I don't like being a sonofabitch. I don't want to be a sonofabitch with you. Don't make me throw you overboard right now!'

The Magician stood over GG and picked him up by the shirt. GG was terrified:

'Hey, hey, just a minute, please. I won't write anything about Cuba. I'll go quietly back home and I won't remember anything. I already had a seat reserved to leave at six. Please.'

'That's what I want to hear. Of course you can come here whenever you like. Especially to play

147

roulette. I saw you a few nights ago in the casino at the Hotel Nacional. Do you like roulette?'

'Yes. And horse racing. I went to Oriental Park a couple of times.'

'That's good. Come whenever you want, bring a lot of money and have fun. But don't write a single line. I've warned you. Next time I won't be talking. When I get tired of talking, I do my magic tricks.'

The Magician stood up. He told the skipper to head back. He sat on the seat in the stern and threw out a line to fish while they approached the shore. They were going at half-speed, not hurrying.

When GG reached the quay, he was overcome by a wave of peace and tranquillity. He looked back and bid a polite farewell to his hosts, but they did not return his gesture. They no longer knew him. Alongside the quay was a bar-restaurant: La Terraza. It had a platform on stilts with tables and a roof. It was a fresh and pleasant place and, at that hour of the day, it was also quiet. GG felt hungry. It was scarcely eight in the morning. He sat in La Terraza and had a ham and cheese sandwich, a glass of orange and a coffee with milk. He knew that in a place like this there would be no point in asking for tea.

He looked at the four crew members of the *Black Sky* who were leaving the yacht. GG opened the manuscript of *The Quiet American* and pretended to read it. Out of the corner of his eye he saw them getting into two cars and disappearing.

GG shut his eyes and breathed deeply. He caught the smell of salt and iodine, and the breeze coming from the blue-green sea. He looked around. Cojímar was a very quiet and peaceful spot. Just fishermen living there. A mini-paradise. 'Paradise awaits you in Cuba'. He got up. He paid his bill. He found a taxi and headed to the airport.

Havana, 2001–2002

Author's/Translator's Note

The extracts quoted from *The Quiet American* are taken from the 1967 Penguin edition, Harmondsworth, Middlesex.

The letter from the Director of the CIA to Fulgencio Batista is in the archive of the Museum of the Ministerio del Interior de Cuba and is transcribed in Enrique Cirules, *The Mafia in Havana: a Caribbean Mob Story*, Ocean Press, Melbourne, New York, 2004, pp.106–7

The quotation from 'The Virtue of Disloyalty' is taken, in part, from the lecture that GG gave at the University of Hamburg in 1969, and is published in Graham Greene, *Reflections*, Viking, New York, 1990, pp.266–70.